Friedrich Halm, Elizabeth Prentiss

## Griselda

A Dramatic Poem in Five Acts

Friedrich Halm, Elizabeth Prentiss

**Griselda**
*A Dramatic Poem in Five Acts*

ISBN/EAN: 9783337375676

Printed in Europe, USA, Canada, Australia, Japan

Cover: Foto ©Andreas Hilbeck / pixelio.de

More available books at **www.hansebooks.com**

# GRISELDA:

# A DRAMATIC POEM

## IN FIVE ACTS.

TRANSLATED FOR THE Y. W. C. A.

FROM THE GERMAN OF
## FRIEDRICH HALM,
(BARON MÜNCH-BELLINGHAUSEN,)

BY
## MRS. E. PRENTISS.

PUBLISHED BY
THE YOUNG WOMEN'S CHRISTIAN ASSOCIATION,
7 EAST FIFTEENTH STREET, NEW YORK.

# PERSONS.

KING ARTHUR.

KENNETH OF SCOTLAND,

LANCELOT, a Frenchman,

GAWAIN,

PERCIVAL OF WALES,

TRISTAN THE WISE,

> Knights of the Round Table.

THE KING'S SENESCHAL.

RONALD, Percival's servant.

CEDRIC, a charcoal-burner (called collier for sake of euphony.)

A BOY.

GINEVRA, wife of King Arthur.

ORIANA,

MERCIA,

> Her Maids of Honor.

ELLINOR, wife of Kenneth.

GRISELDA, Cedric's daughter, wife of Percival.

KNIGHTS AND LADIES.

PERCIVAL'S VASSALS.

GRISELDA'S WOMEN.

*N. B. The author having, occasionally, varied his metre, it was thought best to follow him in the English version.*

# GRISELDA.

## FIRST ACT.

KING ARTHUR'S *castle in Karduel—A brilliantly illuminated, highly ornamented saloon—In the background, music—In the foreground, a throne under a canopy.*

SCENE I. — *Richly-dressed Servants and Pages hasten across the stage with golden cups and glasses—Knights and Ladies move up and down in showy garments, among them* KING ARTHUR, *the* SENESCHAL, TRISTAN THE WISE, PERCIVAL OF WALES.

KING ARTHUR *approaches the* SENESCHAL.

### KING ARTHUR.

I AM well pleased, most worthy Seneschal!
Thou rob'st from night the shimmer of its stars,
From the damp sea the silvery gleam of pearls,
From the earth's bosom the carbuncle's glow,
This festival with splendor to adorn :
I have no more to ask, I am content.

(1)

### SENESCHAL.

No lesser pomp I thought beseeméd, Sire,
The royal host, beseemed the royal guests,
Who, of this kingdom, are the pith and flower;
For see, not one of all thy knights has failed;
Ev'n Percival, the son of forest rude,
Leaves, at thy call, the bosom of the wilds
And ventures in the palace of his king,
To wear the shaggy bear-skin on his shoulders,
And the rough doublet from the buffalo won.

### KING ARTHUR.

What of his robe!   A warrior's scars adorn him,
Bright as the stars he shines in his renown.
Far from my court three years have seen him absent;
And he is welcome, even in a bear-skin.
But now away! too long our guests await us!
Inspire the servants' footsteps, do not suffer
The melody of music's sighs to die.
The wine-cup's golden ground let no man see,
And only let this feast's gay tumult cease
When daylight dawns apace.

### SENESCHAL.

On that depend!
Daylight, alone, shall desolate this hall.

[KING ARTHUR *and the* SENESCHAL *disappear
among the guests. In the meantime* PERCI-
VAL *and* TRISTAN *come forward.*

### PERCIVAL.

Know you yon lady upon Kenneth's arm,
Who sweeps the flooring with her satin's hem,
While the proud heron's feather on her head
Reaches the gilded wainscot of this hall?

### TRISTAN.

It is Dame Ellinor, and Kenneth's wife,
From Fingal's ancient, royal race she sprang,
And unrestrained as Fingal over Erin,
In Kenneth's house the royal sceptre bears.

### PERCIVAL.

And he, poor simpleton, the sceptre yields her?
Wears he no doublet but a woman's gown?
And who, with magic wand and girdle, yonder
In dreary meditation silent broods,
As to this throng a stranger; who is she?

### TRISTAN.

'Tis the king's sister; she is called Morgana,
For her great knowledge she is world-renowned,

And for her insight into hidden things;
In the black art 'tis even said she deals.

### PERCIVAL.

Better for her in household arts to deal!
Silent obedience from my wife I claim,
Submission to her husband's despot law:
Wisdom, like strength, is our inheritance,
And but a plaything in a woman's hand.

### TRISTAN.

A plaything, Percival?

### PERCIVAL.

Yes, Tristan, yes!
Would you a woman picture to the life,
Just as the Lord for our refreshment made her?
She sits and spins; unto her swelling breast
She fondly clasps her child; her pious glance
Devoutly turns away from earth to heaven.
What this transcends is but superfluous.
What time is it?

### TRISTAN.

'Tis very nearly midnight.

### PERCIVAL.

It wearies me, this feast, would it were over!

### TRISTAN.

How, Percival, this hall in royal splendor,
These joyous guests in this enticing throng
Delight you not?  Breathes forth for you in vain
The fragrance of this air? in vain for you
The Siren song of music?  Discontent
You nurse amid this regal, noon-tide glow?

### PERCIVAL.

That do I, Sir!  At Pendennys, my home,
Halls in my castle also shine and sparkle.
And when I bid them, guests come thither also,
And also gape, astonished at my wealth,
And pay their court to me!  What do I here?
Bending my back, and bowing down my knee,
Who am a monarch in my own domain!

### TRISTAN.

Well see I, Percival, you long for home;
Long for your faithful wife and for your child.

### PERCIVAL.

What say you?  How?

### TRISTAN.

I say it is your pleasure
To sit at Pendennys with wife and child.

### PERCIVAL.

What? Slew I Cathmor not, not Swen the Dane?
Am I not Percival? Does not my name
Resound, with honor, through this island green,
Where Giant-killer I am proudly called?

### TRISTAN.

Truly, they call thee so.

### PERCIVAL.

And you, Sir Tristan,
You think a lady's maid I have become,
Who by the cradle sits, keeps off the flies,
And meekly makes jack-puddings for the child?
St. David, Sir! But I a wife have taken,
Not a wife me!

### TRISTAN.

And what is wanting, then?
Why knit the wrinkled brow as thunder clouds
Portentous gather?

### PERCIVAL.

I myself know not !
It vexes me that I am satisfied;
The day's insipid sweetness makes me thirst
For gall and wormwood; as the worn-out palate
Desires the sharpest flavors, so my temper,
Weary of what is charming, yearns for rudeness.

### TRISTAN.

Ah, Percival, you know not what you want !

### PERCIVAL.

Perhaps so; yet I want it !   In our country
There is a stream—the Trent, we Welshmen call it;
It takes its source amid the mountains high,
And noisily flows sparkling through the land.
Now mark my words: the while its foaming water
Winds its way toiling through the valley's clefts,
Rushes o'er stones, and breaks through mountain-passes,
Making its banks to tremble with its roar;
So long like liquid crystal it is clear,
Full of young life and of unbroken strength;
It carries grains of gold within its bosom,
And trout sport gaily in its cool embrace.
Yet if from out the mountain's lap it ventures,

Over the corn-fields runs unlimited,
And like a wide sea spreads abroad its arms,
It creeps with languor through its marshy bed,
With scarce a murmur, bows beneath the bridge,
Obeys the rudder, turns the miller's wheel,
And toads and snakes amid its slime find shelter.

### TRISTAN.

You mean then—

### PERCIVAL.

   Ay, and swear it by mine oath !
That I hold kinship with the river Trent,
And was not born the household wheels to turn ;
And were my faithful wife in virtue richer,
And, mark me, Sir, a faithful wife is she,
If she wore angels' wings upon her shoulders,
A wife, a child alone, this bosom fills not !
But come, Sir Tristan, yet a parting cup,
And then for home !

### TRISTAN.

So early, Percival ?

### PERCIVAL.

If not at once, then surely ere 'tis morning.

        [*They go off.*

SCENE II.–*Loud music in the background*—GINEVRA *appears, heated from the dance*—LANCELOT *accompanies her*—*They are followed at some distance by* ORIANA, MERCIA, GAWAIN *and other Knights and Ladies*—*In the background are* KENNETH *and* ELLINOR.

### LANCELOT.

Torture me not; you madden me, Ginevra !
As the hot sun the verdant meadow scorches,
So with a glance dost thou my brain consume,
And wither up and waste away my thoughts.
How can I bear with thine inconstancy ?
Thy smiles are falsehoods, and thy tears are lies;
Thine anger's favor, and thy kindness hate.
Who understands—has ever understood thee ?
Oh, if thou knewest what a wealth of love
This heart conceals !

### GINEVRA.

Speak lower, Lancelot!

### GAWAIN (*to* MERCIA).

By those star-lighted eyes, I ask it, Mercia
Say, hate you me ?
1*

### MERCIA.

Oh, no !

### GAWAIN.

You love me, then ?

### MERCIA.

Oh, no !

### GAWAIN.

Have you no milder word for me ?
Spake never then within your bosom's depth,
A longing sweet, a wish mysterious ?

### MERCIA.

Oh, yes !

### GAWAIN.

Well, give it word and voice then !
Speak, Mercia, speak ; your heart unfold to me !

### MERCIA.

I fain would marry, Sir !

### GAWAIN (*aside*).

Well now, good heavens !
What leaky vessels these young creatures are !

### GINEVRA.

Nay, you deceive me not! Some pleasant pictures,
Like fleeting dreams, pass lightly o'er our souls,
But disappear as doth the morning dew!
Truth lies in hatred, but lies not in love.

### LANCELOT.

When thus love's power thou heartlessly deniest, ·
As with a gloomy pall thou shroudest life,
And snatchest from the heart the bloom of May.
> [*He continues to converse, in a low tone, with* GIN-
> EVRA, *while* KENNETH *and* ELLINOR *appear
> in the foreground.*

### ELLINOR.

Do not expect, Sir Kenneth, to deceive me!
What did you say to Lady Morgana,
When you within the window's recess sought her?

### KENNETH.

I, Ellinor?

### ELLINOR.
Yes, you, will you deny it?

### KENNETH.

Deny it? No! Indeed I'll not deny it!

Of the black art she prated unto me,
About the pathway of the stars and planets,
Till she her thread's discourse, I patience lost.
Would that she sat, herself, on one of them!

### ELLINOR.

Perfidious man!   And I, this nursery tale,
This silly, downright falsehood, shall believe?
Once safe at home, and you shall pay for this!

### GAWAIN.

What ails you, Kenneth?   Say, are you not well?
You're shivering as if you had a fever.

### KENNETH.

'Tis nothing but a buzzing in my ears, Sir!

### GINEVRA (*to* LANCELOT).

No farther, Lancelot!   There slumbers poison,
And death broods in the honey of your words!
I will hear nothing more!   I'm weary now,
And for repose I long.

### LANCELOT.

Here is a seat
Right royally adorned, thou gracious one,

Worthy the Queen of Beauty to receive.

> [*He leads her to a throne, around which the
> Knights and Ladies gradually gather.*

### GINEVRA.

Nay, do not leave us yet, Sir Lancelot!
You are my knight, be seated at my feet!
Now, noble ladies, heroes of renown,
Approach, and let our moments of repose
With cheerful conversation be lit up.
But, first of all, pray who among you knows
The knight who by the sideboard is entrenched,
The sunburnt knight, with black and curling locks?

### ORIANA (*glibly*).

Do you mean Walladmor, who to his rivals
From his beloved bore her messages?
Or think you of the slender Lionel
Who wed his blooming spring to Signa's winter,
And pays such homage to her fading charms?

### GINEVRA.

Not he!

### ORIANA.

Ah, then, you think of Ethelrich,

Who seven years long wooed Mildred, until she
Took to herself Westmoreland in the eighth;
Close at his side there sits Sir Josalin,
And reckons up how many hides of land*
His wife is wearing in her hair to-night.
And next him comes—

### GINEVRA.

       Quite right, thou naughty babbler;
And next him, clad in bear-skin, comes a knight,
Who unadorned this festal scene insults.

### ORIANA.

Oh, that is Percival, your royal highness;
The Giant-killer called throughout the land.

### GAWAIN (*to* GINEVRA).

What, know you not this hero, so renowned?

### GINEVRA.

His name and person were unknown to me.

### ORIANA.

And how, my gracious lady, should you know him?

---

* The ancient way of measuring land by strips of leather.

Since he has tak'n a wife into his home,
For years from the king's court he has withdrawn,
And deep within the dusky forest dwelt.


KENNETH.

He has a wife ?

LANCELOT.

What, Percival is married ?
Could he, more proud than mighty or renowned,
Not find a lady worthy of his hand
Within King Arthur's court ?


ORIANA.

Quite right, the same.


ELLINOR.

He who the royal blood too watery fancied
To mingle with the torrent of his own ?


ORIANA.

Yes, this is Percival, the very same !


GINEVRA.

And of what lineage is she ?   Answer that.

### ORIANA.

From the Welsh mountains no report we have
Of his wife's name or of her lineage.

### GINEVRA.

He is approaching : what if I should ask ?

### ORIANA.

I'll ask him, Queen.   You may depend on me !

---

SCENE III. — PERCIVAL, TRISTAN, *and the* QUEEN'S
party.

### PERCIVAL.

By heaven !   I never knew a milder fire
Than this new, fragrant wine has waked in me !
My pulses fly, my face is all aglow,
And every hidden secret of my soul,
Ready for flight, sits wingéd on my lips.
Yet 'mid this crowd of courtiers what do I ?
In festal garments clad, they stand arrayed,
Courting applause, and prattling pretty things !
I think we're breaking up !

TRISTAN.

Ah, Percival,
The blackest darkness in the valleys broods ;
Not before morning dare I homeward ride.

GINEVRA.

Sir Percival !

PERCIVAL.

Who calls ?

TRISTAN.

It is Ginevra,
It is the Queen, she beckons you ; step nearer.

GINEVRA.

Sir Percival, pray will you not acquaint us
With her, who you, th' invincible, o'ercame ?

PERCIVAL.

What mean you, Queen ?

GINEVRA.

I mean, Sir, are you married ?

PERCIVAL.

Who says so ?

GINEVRA.

Are you not ?


PERCIVAL.

              Of course I am !
You think I am ashamed to own it ?   Nay !
My wife, Griselda, shall I then deny ?
With fairer wife this earth was ne'er adorned,
And yet her beauty is her smallest charm ;
For she is pious, humble as a flower,
Of lamb-like patience, full of grace and truth,
Simple and plain, yet full of life and soul ;
I have known many women, ne'er a better !
What though a charcoal-burner is her father,
What though no noble blood is in her veins ?


GINEVRA (*half aloud to those about her, as all the rest who
                   follow*).
Can it be ?


ORIANA.

Shameful !


GAWAIN.

But a charcoal-burner !

### ELLINOR.

How my head swims! This is a perfect outrage!
Thus is our old nobility profaned?

### GINEVRA.

Sir Gawain, follow Percival's example;
So end your woman-hatred.

### GAWAIN.

Oh, your highness,
Could I first hate, soon could I turn to love;
But with a coat of mail experience arms me,
And marriage is a very serious thing!
Is it not so, fair Mercia?

### MERCIA.

Yes; oh, yes!

### GAWAIN.

You surely would not take a smutty coalman?

### MERCIA.

Oh, no!

### PERCIVAL (*to* TRISTAN).

What's going on among them there?

Why whisper they together, and why laugh ?
Saint David !   Is't of me ?

### TRISTAN.

Ay, Percival !
You know the ways of women !   Have you never
Heard them talk nonsense with an air of wisdom ?
Let them alone !   What can they be to you ?

### GINEVRA (*to those about her.*)

You wish it ?   Well, then, I will undertake it !
Sir Percival, pray our regret imagine,
Not to behold this master-piece, Griselda !
Wherefore have you forbid her coming hither ?

### PERCIVAL.

Not my command, but her own wish restrained her ;
She stays at home and watches o'er her boy.

### GENEVRA.

Oh, soft maternal heart, that gives completeness
To her rare virtues by this consecration !
But since we lose the pleasure of her presence,
Prithee declare to us by what strange luck
So rich a treasure to your hand was given ?

### PERCIVAL.

My Queen, if really you desire to hear it,
I'm not ashamed to tell the story truly ;
I'm my own master, wherefore should I not ?

### GINEVRA.

Begin, Sir Percival !

### PERCIVAL.

        Your royal highness,
Three years ago, my people, with petitions
Urgent and oft-repeated, overwhelmed me,
At once by marriage to preserve my race,
And from estrangement keep my heritage.
But in this royal court full oft I'd thrown
A curious glance into the female heart;
I found it spiteful, false, and treacherous,
Defiant of restraint, disdainful, bold,
Full of conceit, yet without faith or strength,
Shameless in its abuse of manly trust,
And shameless also in unbridled lusts ;
Finding none worthy, therefore, of my choice,
Love died within me, thought of marriage died,
Nor do I now repent me of the loss.

ELLINOR (*in a half whisper.*)

With his rude speech compared, his doublet's soft!


ORIANA.

Insolent wretch!


GINEVRA.

               But he shall pay for this!
(*To* LANCELOT, *who steps angrily forward.*)
No farther, Lancelot! Sir Percival,
Continue!


PERCIVAL.

               Upon a summer evening
The hunt had to the forest green enticed me,
In deep dejection, with myself at war;
My gloomy breast with restless fancies full,
I wandered slowly on, nor marked the path,
My careless footsteps leading me astray;
Until the silvery waters of a brook
That through this forest wanders, checked my steps!
Then I looked up and saw, I saw, oh Queen!
A maiden in unearthly beauty clad,
Yet all unconscious of her loveliness;
A maiden on whose brow was written, Queen,

In letters from an alphabet of stars,
That God in heaven, when He fashioned her,
Smiled softly, saying, Perfect have I made thee!
This maiden, now my wife, your Majesty,
Stood by the brookside, lost in pleasant thought.

GINEVRA (*aside to her party.*)

No doubt she took a bath, hoping to cleanse her
From smut unseemly off her father's coals.

ORIANA.

Not so, my lady!   For suppose the water
Should wash away th' inscription from her forehead,
That said God made her gloriously perfect?
She would not risk it!

PERCIVAL (*to* TRISTAN.)
     They turn up their noses,
And with grimaces sly, look hitherward!
Saint David! Tristan, they are mocking me!

TRISTAN.

Nay, Percival, you make too much of it!
Let them amuse themselves with pastime poor;
Why vex yourself?

PERCIVAL.

Plague take these women's tongues!

GINEVRA (*to her party.*)

Control your wit and mirth, compose your faces,
That longer yet this pastime may amuse us!
Now, Percival, proceed!

PERCIVAL.

What was I saying?
I have it now! Beside the brook she stood;
Her dusky hair hung rippling round her face,
And perched upon her shoulders sat a dove;
Right home-like sat she there, her wings scarce moving.
Now suddenly she stoops—I mean the maiden—
Down to the spring, and lets her little feet
Sink in its waters, while her colored skirt
Covered with care what they did not conceal;
And I within the shadows of the trees,
Inly admired her graceful modesty.
And as she sat and gazed into the brook,
Plashing and sporting with her snow-white feet,
She thought not of the olden times, when girls
Pleased to behold their faces smiling back
From the smooth water, used it as their mirror

By which to deck themselves and plait their hair;
But like a child she sat with droll grimaces,
Delighted when the brook gave back to her
Her own distorted charms; so then I said:
Conceited is she not.

### KENNETH.

                              The charming child!

### ELLINOR.

What is a collier's child to you!   By heaven!
Don't make me fancy that you know her, Sir!

### PERCIVAL.

And now resounding through the mountain far,
From the church-tower rang forth the vesper-bell,
And she grew grave and still, and shaking quickly
From off her face the hair that fell around it,
She cast a thoughtful and angelic glance
Upward, where clouds had caught the evening red,
And her lips gently moved with whispered words,
As rose-leaves tremble when the soft winds breathe.
O she is saintly, flashed it through my soul;
She marking on her brow the holy cross,
Lifted her face, bright with the sunset's flush,

2

While holy longing and devotion's glow
Moistened her eye and hung like glory round her.
Then to her breast the little dove she clasped,
Embraced, caressed it, kissed its snow-white wings,
And laughed, when with its rose-red bill, it pecked,
As if with longing for her fresh young lips.
How she'd caress it, said I to myself,
Were this her child, the offspring of her love!
And now a voice resounded through the woods,
And cried, " Griselda," cried it, " Come, Griselda ! "
While she, the distant voice's sound distinguished,
Sprang quickly up, and scarcely lingering
Her feet to dry, ran up the dewy bank
With lightning speed, her dove in circles o'er her,
Till in the dusky thicket disappeared
For me the last edge of her flutt'ring robe.
" Obedient is she," said I to myself;
And many things revolving, turned I home.

### Ginevra.

By heaven ! You tell your tale so charmingly,
And with such warmth and truth to life, the hearer
Out of your words can shape a human form.
Why, I can see this loveliest of maidens
Sit by the brook-side making her grimaces;

They are right pretty faces spite of coal-smut.
Is it not so, Sir Percival?


ORIANA (*aside to the Queen.*)
My lady!
Behold, I beg you, how his veins are swelling,
And how with crimson glow his fiery cheeks.


GENEVRA (*to* ORIANA.)

His hairy doublet he perhaps repents!


PERCIVAL (*to* TRISTAN.)

Would with a look that I could poison her!
I swell with anger, am consumed with rage.


TRISTAN.

Control yourself; heed not their childish prattle,
And take not counsel of your angry blood.


PERCIVAL (*aside.*)

I'll bide my time, then, and that time will come!
Your royal highness!  All my serfs and vassals
Gathered before my castle at my call;
And high upon my horse, in festal throng,

I rode to greet once more the dusky glade
The verdant cradle of Griselda's charms,
With waving banners and resounding horns.
Before her hut my band of vassals halted,
And I, alone, the lowly threshold crossed.
She sat between her parents, open-browed,
Clear-eyed ; her blind old father stroked her cheeks,
Her gray-haired mother sported with her hair ;
That she to them was all in all, I saw.
With quick decision I before her stood.
" Griselda," spake I, " tell me, canst thou love me ?"
With glance intelligent she saw and proved me,
And deeply blushing, nodded with her head.
And further yet I asked : "Wilt thou, Griselda,
Forsake thy parents, give thyself to me ?"
And she said, " Yes !"  And then I asked her further :
" Wilt thou to me obedience show, Griselda,
As to thy master?" and she said, " I will!"
Ah ! then I pressed a kiss upon her lips,
The gray-haired parents blessed their only child,
And in  my own strong arms I bore her forth,
Where all my vassals waited me without ;
" Behold your mistress !" cried I, " see my bride !"
Then shrilly pealed the horns, and jubilees
Resounded through the ranks ; I took her home.

A priestly benediction made us one,
And so, your royal highness, I was wed!

### GINEVRA.

Sir, we congratulate you! May your love
Forever flame and glow like burning coals!

### ELLINOR.

May one inquire, most worthy Percival,
How many bags of coal your fair one brought you,
As bridal gift?

### ORIANA.

She brought him nothing more
Than the full heart of love he sought from her,
And that well carbonized with hot desire!

### ELLINOR.

Sir Percival, might one a counsel give you?
Have painted, as memorial of your choice,
A charcoal-burner's pole upon your banner!

### GINEVRA.

Ah, tell me if your wife still makes grimaces?
And puffs her cheeks out? How they must become her!

Enough of jests !   Sir Percival, farewell.
Bear to your collier's child Ginevra's greeting !

*[Is about to go.*

PERCIVAL (*enraged*).
Poison and dagger, plague and leprosy,
Rather than speak thy name !

TRISTAN.
You've lost your senses !

LANCELOT.
This cries for blood !

PERCIVAL.
It does !   And you shall shed it !

*[ They draw.*

GINEVRA.
I'm fainting !

*[She supports herself on* ORIANA—TRISTAN, *and
other Knights step between the combatants.*

TRISTAN.
Part them !

GAWAIN.
Stay !   Disarm them !

PERCIVAL.
Back !

SCENE IV.—*The* SENESCHAL *steps forward, followed by*
　KING ARTHUR.

### SENESCHAL.

Give way, my masters all, and keep the peace!
This castle is the King's!　Back, gentlemen!

PERCIVAL (*who in the meantime has shaken off all the
　　　Knights who restrained him.*)
Out of the way, old fool, with thy white staff!
Come on, Sir Lancelot!

KING ARTHUR (*seizing* PERCIVAL *by the arm*).
Hold, say I, hold!
[*The music ceases, the other guests approach, astonished.*
Why trouble you my brilliant festival,
And the sweet clangor of the music deafen
With battle-cries, and noisy din of arms?
What is it, Lancelot?　Speak, Percival!
What is the quarrel?

### PERCIVAL.

Ask Ginevra, yonder!

### GINEVRA.

My Lord and King! The boldest arrogance
Lightly esteeming all our sacred rights,
Has wounded and insulted me, thy Queen,
Within thy castle.

### KING ARTHUR.

                    What! thou speakest truly?

### ORIANA.

Truly so was it, Sire! With fury burning,
At passing words and harmless, playful jests,
With shameful language he approached the Queen,
And gradually thence arose this strife.

### KING ARTHUR.

And it is really so? Speak, Percival!

### PERCIVAL.

With rough words, truly, I addressed her, Sire ;
By scorn excited, goaded by contempt,
When she my wife contemnéd for her birth,
When she the mother of my child insulted,
And every sacred impulse of my heart
Made despicable by her empty wit;

That did I, Sire, and injured thus again,
Now, by my father's beard, I would repeat them!

### KING ARTHUR.

Thou of this castle hast profaned the halls,
And in my wife thou hast offended me,
Thy Lord and King; the lustre of the crown
Is tarnished by the breath of thy bold mouth.

### PERCIVAL.

Saint David!   Sire, why slandered she my wife?
What if a collier's child, the forest bore her,
Yet is she modest, faithful, full of love,
Richer in true adornment of the soul
Than any other wife could boast before her;
Not one of you, ye proud and high-born dames,
Was carvéd out from nobler wood than she,
And though you flaunt in many-colored rags,
Not one is equal to the collier's child,
Ay, by mine oath, not one, I say, not one!

### ORIANA.

Audacious braggart!   You insult the Queen!

### TRISTAN (*to* PERCIVAL).

You go beyond all bounds; come to your senses!

2*

PERCIVAL (*to the* QUEEN, *who with difficulty conceals her anger*).

What angers thee, O Queen ?   I tremble not
Before the darts of thy majestic glance !
Not I !   And here before them all, I say
If worth and justice reigned upon this earth,
She whom thou scornest, she would be the Queen,
And thou wouldst kneel before the collier's child !

GINEVRA (*to* KING ARTHUR).

And such a gross affront you bear in silence,
And I must bear it, also ?

KING ARTHUR.

      Peace, Ginevra !
Not one word, Percival !   Now, by my kingdom !
Injustice weighs alike on either side,
And neither party should itself forgive :
Only this outraged realm atonement asks,
This castle's injured rights demand it also :
Thou therefore, Percival, must penance do ;
Yet mild and lenient shall thy sentence be,
Gladly we will forgive and glad forget :
Only retract thy words !

### PERCIVAL.

Retract them!   No!

Not I!

### KING ARTHUR.

And by mine oath, retract thou shalt!

### PERCIVAL.

And by mine oath, the heavens first shall fall!

### GINEVRA (*after some moments' reflection*).

Permit me now to speak, my Lord and King!
Let him unloose the knots who them entangled!
Sir Percival, you'll not retract your words,
And I will kneel before the collier's child.

### PERCIVAL.

What say you?

### LANCELOT.

Wonderful!

### ELLINOR.

She speaks at random!

### KING ARTHUR.

Ginevra, art thou jesting?

GINEVRA.

Let me finish !
I kneel, Sir Knight, before the collier's child,
When you full proof can give me, that your wife
So faithful, virtuous, and lovely is,
So consecrate to you and to your weal,
That if on earth the good and true took rank,
She should be Queen and wear proud England's crown !
If this you prove, then will I kneel to her.

PERCIVAL.

You will then ?

GINEVRA.
Yes, I will !

KING ARTHUR.
What, Percival,
Will you to doubtful strife a question leave,
When one repentant word would peace restore ?

PERCIVAL.

And what for proofs and tests demand you, Queen ?

GINEVRA.

First, I demand that you require your wife

To give to you the boy that she has borne,
To be delivered to your feudal-lord,
Who both rejects your marriage and its fruits,
And threatens banishment if you refuse !

### PERCIVAL.

She loves her child, with her whole soul she loves it,
But me she loves yet more !   She'd give her life,
She'd give her child for me !   Shall I retract ?
What more demand you, Queen ?

### GINEVRA.

            And further, Sir,
Demand I from you to disown your wife
In open hall before your feudataries,
Sending her helpless, poor, and naked from you,
As helpless, poor, and naked you received her.

### PERCIVAL.

And further, Queen ?

### GINEVRA.

            And as for your Griselda,
Although her soul is wounded to its depths,
She undiminished tenderness shall bear you ;

Her glowing love shall not to hatred turn,
Her gentle patience into bitterness;
Yes, your affronts shall bind you to her closer
Than when at first you clasped her as your bride.

PERCIVAL.

And then?

GINEVRA.

Then will Ginevra kneel before Griselda!
But if she fail, if from this test by fire
She come not spotless forth, like purest gold,
Then, Percival, thou at my feet shalt kneel!

PERCIVAL.

The very poles shall kiss each other first!

KING ARTHUR.

Humble your haughtiness, Sir Percival!
If a retraction wounds you, yet more deeply
The torture of these tests will wound Griselda.

GINEVRA.

Why hesitate? Decide, Sir Percival!

### PERCIVAL.

You fancy I am frightened at your tests?
Griselda will come forth victorious;
I am as sure of it as had she done so!
Listen; her father, Cedric is his name,
A charcoal-burner, blind, advanced in years,
But rough, inflexible, and quarrelsome,
With me contended for the mastery,
And since his pride refused me homage due,
Furious with rage I showed him to the door.
Griselda saw it, and she wept, O Queen!
She wept, but she was silent! Would you more?
A year ago, perhaps, I lay exhausted
By serious wounds and very nigh to death.
At the same time Griselda's mother sickened,
And fain would bless her in her parting hour;
But she, oppressed with care, and comfortless,
Not a foot's length would venture from my couch
Till I was cured. Meanwhile the mother died,
And saw her child no more! And I shall tremble?
I enter on the contest safely, Queen!
I am her all, the victory is mine!

### ORIANA.

First win the victory, then rejoice in it!

TRISTAN.

Griselda's love has verified the deed ;
Be not by cunning trickery enticed.
Retract, Sir Percival !

PERCIVAL (*aside.*)

                    What cutting pain,
What bitter grief her heart will penetrate,
When she essays this testing path of thorns ;
Yet for my sake her courage will not quail,
And she shall show what love can do and bear.
The question, Queen, you will decide by strife ;
Well, let it be so !   Combat shall decide !

KING ARTHUR.

Then you consent ?

TRISTAN.

                    Unhappy man, retract !

KING ARTHUR.

Reflect on your decision, Percival ;
To spare yourself a single drop of gall,
You give it in full measure to your wife !
Act not from impulse, follow better counsel ;
Time for reflection we will gladly give !

PERCIVAL.

My knightly word is valid for all times!

GINEVRA.

Two knights, then, will be chosen by the King,
And go as escorts with you to your home,
That all unwarned, Griselda's vaunted worth
May shine upon them in unsullied light;
Nor shall the trial end, the gloomy problem
Be solved till I, myself, shall lift the veil;
Promise you this?

PERCIVAL.

I promise it, your highness!

KING ARTHUR.

You follow your own will, then, Percival!
Gawain and Tristan shall escort you home!
Depart in peace.

PERCIVAL.

I bid you, Sire, farewell,
We're breaking up!  To horse!  To horse, my comrades!
The morning dawns, and ere the stars grow pale,

Pendennys' friendly walls shall welcome us.

        *[Departs with* GAWAIN *and* TRISTAN.

### KING ARTHUR.

Ginevra, come !   We'll bring to a conclusion
A festival by discord so embittered !
Yet with the morrow hasten to Pendennys,
And bring this gloomy mummery to an end ;
The hunt will lead me into yonder vales ;
I hope that I may find you reconciled :
Love for the sins of pride  should not atone !

### GINEVRA (*aside to* ORIANA.)

Down in the dust he at my feet shall kneel !

# SECOND ACT.

*Castle Pendennys—It is night: a lamp dimly lights up the scene, which represents a vaulted, richly-carved apartment—The main entrance is in the background; on the left is a side-door.*

### SCENE I.—GRISELDA *enters on the left.*

#### GRISELDA.

What can detain him? Dusky sinks the night,
In a grey veil the pale moon hides away
Her faded face; damp fogs and vapors rise
Dismally from the Trent! What can detain him?
May no misfortune hinder his return!
But listen! Hark! With steps the halls resound;
I hear the door! 'Tis he! You're welcome, Ronald,
I've waited for thee long!

#### RONALD.

    My gracious lady!
The lowering weather makes a gloomy night;
The sky is covered with such heavy clouds

That oftentimes I could not see the path,
And the thick darkness every step impeded.

### GRISELDA.

Bring you a message ?   Tell me, have you seen him—
My blind old father, venerated man ?

### RONALD.

Not distant from his hut I found him, lady,
Where the old oak 'mid seas of foliage stands ;
Upon the moss reclining found I him,
And near him lay the boy, his guide and guard.

### GRISELDA.

And as my mediator didst thou act,
And turn his anger into love and grace ?

### RONALD.

Lady, full well thou knowest him thyself,
Easy to anger, hard to reconcile.
Gravely and mildly he received my greeting,
For friendly towards me was he wont to be ;
But when thy message I to him made known
His brow was darkened as with stormy clouds ;
About his lips there played a bitter smile ;

Go, cried he, tell the wife of Percival,
No more the collier shall the threshold cross
Of yonder castle ; never shall the roof
Of Pendennys his head presume to shade,
Whom pride has banished from his daughter's arms,
Whom she, unfilial, hurries to his grave.

### GRISELDA.

Was it then I, his child, who banished him ?
It was Sir Percival, his lord and mine,
And yet not he ; a moment unpropitious,
The passing humor of a gloomy hour,
Forced from his lips alone that hasty word.

### RONALD.

And so I told him ; he, however, lady,
With angry gestures made this harsh reply :
"What she did not, she suffered to be done ;
She could look on and see my banishment ;
She could find tears, but words she could not find !"

### GRISELDA.

Oh heaven, could I but with silent tears,
The bitter wrath of Percival oppose !
Submission only could appease his rage !

I suffered what I could not change, to be ;
But God, but God, my agony could see.


### RONALD.

So told I him, yet darker, blacker yet
Became the angry cloud upon his brow.
Then spake he thus : " Much, much I would forgive ;
Yet this forgive I not ; she let her mother,
Who, dying, yearned once more to see her child,
Yearn for her vainly ; for her blessing came not ;
The mother died, and saw her child no more !"


### GRISELDA.

And for my husband, lay not Death in ambush
As for my mother ?   Dared I to forsake him ?
To hands of hirelings heartlessly entrust him ?
What my soul suffered in those days of care
I only know ; the fear and the despair,
The eager filial longing, filial love,
That with the wife's affection fiercely strove,
That saw He only who counts up our tears.


### RONALD.

That, too, I told him, lady ; he, however—

### GRISELDA.

Why hesitate ?   Speak out !   What wouldst conceal ?

### RONALD.

Far better, lady, were it to be silent ;
'Tis a hard word the final word he spake ;
'Twill wound thee deeply.

### GRISELDA.

> Yet conceal it not !

### RONALD.

Thus, with distorted features, spake he then,
His face inflamed and glowing with its rage ;
"A curse," he cried, " a curse on your proud name,
And curses on the pomp and pride of rank !
They stole my child from me !   For empty show,
A troop of servants, and for glittering gold
She learned the collier's hovel to disdain,
Her mother's dying blessing to despise !"
Speaking these words he gathered up himself,
Seized the boy's arm, motioned me not to follow,
And towards the dusky forest turned his steps.

### GRISELDA.

No, this offence lies not upon my soul !

Not pomp and show, not empty pageantry,
Love only linked my fate with Percival's.
I gave my heart to him to win his own,
Love's the pure gold I craved, and love the gem;
Of his moist eye to catch the pearly shimmer,
Not power to gain, or state, or tinsel glimmer!
Is love a crime?   Well, I am guilty then!
For love's sweet sake I lost my mother's blessing:
Love is my happiness, and love my pride!

### RONALD.

Thou knowest thine innocence!   Take courage then!
Bear thy reproach in patience; trust to time.

### GRISELDA.

And will it ever come, the longed-for time,
That will restore him to his daughter's arms?

### RONALD.

The time will come, and will outrun thy hopes!
Amid these well-known walls his spirit dwells;
With eagerness he asked how this one fared,
How that one found himself, and more than once
He showed parental fondness for the boy.

### GRISELDA.

Is't possible?

### RONALD.

'Tis really so, my lady!
Hope, therefore, for the best; when passion cools,
And to reflection yields, then he will yearn
For the sweet pleasures known in other days;
To see his child, to hear his grandson's voice;
His loving arms he'll open suddenly,
As the firm rock will long remain unshaken,
Until by torrents slowly undermined,
When but a touch will cause its overthrow.

### GRISELDA.

How with the dew of hope thou hast refreshed me,
And soothed my heart with gentle, kindly words!
I thank thee for it; prithee now to rest!

### RONALD.

May God protect you, lady! Sleep in peace! [*Goes off.*

### GRISELDA (*after serious reflection.*)

The mother died and saw her child no more!
Oh, sainted one! If from the heights of heaven
Thou lookest down upon this earthly scene,

Forgavest thou that not thy daughter's hand
Thine eyelids closed, that not within her arms
Thou, dying, didst breathe forth thy parting sigh?
Thou, too, for thy belovéd didst forsake
Thy country and thy home; made a new home,
And was a stranger to thy father's house!
Yes, thou forgavest me the wifely love
That kept me distant from thy dying bed,
Though yearnings vain thy parting hours oppressed,
And of ingratitude thy soul accused me!

     Oh, sharp reproach, suspicion terrible!
Does evil, then, take the pre-eminence,
Even in virtue, e'en in love itself?
And love I him too much? For his whole life,
The undivided treasure of his heart,
Can I give less to him than my whole self,
My heart, my life, my all, unlimited?
Did I not vow eternal love to him?
Is it not duty, is it not delight,
And is it not the highest bliss of earth,
Beloved to love, and loving to make blissful?
Oh, keep thee fast, my heart, unto thy love!
Keep up thy cheerful courage, bear unshaken
Unjust suspicion and thy father's pique,
And make atonement with thy drop of gall,

For the untroubled sweetness of thy love !
              [*She steps thoughtfully to the window.*
A dull obscurity enfolds the valleys,
And stares upon me with its gloomy shades !
I will to bed !   My dearest Percival !
Dost think of me amid the show and glitter
Of the King's castle ?   Yes, thou thinkest of me ;
For as thine image stands before my soul,
Mine also lovingly round thee must hover !
Good-night !   Good-night, beloved Percival !
I'll look upon my child, and then to bed.

    [*She turns to leave by the side door, as* PERCIVAL,
      GAWAIN, *and* TRISTAN *enter by the main
      door.*

---

SCENE II.—PERCIVAL, TRISTAN, GAWAIN, GRISELDA.

PERCIVAL.

Griselda !

GRISELDA (*rushing up to him*).

      Percival !   Thou hast returned !
Once more I see thee, dearest Percival !

PERCIVAL.

Good-evening, my Griselda !

GRISELDA (*in his arms*).

Percival!
Once more I have thee?   Thou wast long away!
Three tedious days!   And hast thou thought of me,
Or to the ladies yonder paid thy court?
No?   Thou hast done it not?   Now nevermore
Shalt thou go forth from me!   Come, kiss me now!
How the hot sunshine has embrowned thy cheeks!
Oh, how at rest I feel upon thy breast,
My Percival!   My lord, my shield, my husband!

PERCIVAL.

But see, Griselda!

GRISELDA.

What keeps thee here?
Think of our Athelstan, our merry boy,
Free from his leading-strings, across the hall,
The child ran safely on, nor stumbled once;
Old Allan wept for joy when he beheld it!
And only think, my little doves are fledged;
Heart-sore was I, and troubled nigh to death,
Not merely missing thee; for other things
Distress and torture me!   But let us see
If thou of mother and of child hast thought,
And what bright gift thou hast brought home to us

From the King's festival? Naught? Hast forgotten?
Thou naughty little father!

### PERCIVAL.

See, Griselda!
I have brought guests with me! Go bid them welcome!
Brave men are they, and Knights of the Round Table,
And hearest thou, Griselda? Worthy friends!

### GRISELDA (*ashamed and blushing*).

I saw him only; pardon, gentlemen!

### TRISTAN.

We ask for yours! The joy of your re-union
Should not be poisoned by our presence here,
Nor full possession of it be denied you.

### PERCIVAL.

A truce, Sir Tristan, to your pretty speeches!
I can assure you, you are welcome here!
Is it not so, Griselda?

### GRISELDA.

Surely, Sirs!
Though you are late, I gladly bid you welcome!
Be pleased to follow me to the saloon.

PERCIVAL.

Not so, we here remain !

GRISELDA.

　　　　　　You'll wake the child ;
He's sleeping near us !   Dost thou wish to kiss him ?

PERCIVAL.

There's time enough for that ; now forth, Griselda !
Give us substantial food, and goblets flowing ;
Hard have we ridden, and it storms without,
As if 'twould sweep away both heaven and earth.
Make haste, Griselda, go !

GRISELDA.

　　　　　　I will, my Lord !
All that the house affords shall soon refresh you ;
I only pray you waken not the child !　　　　　[*Goes.*

———————

SCENE III.—PERCIVAL, TRISTAN, GAWAIN.

PERCIVAL (*who has thrown himself into an arm-chair*).
Once more, ye worthy knights, I bid you welcome
To my poor house, to Castle Pendennys !

That you are truly so, you've seen, methinks.
What think you of the collier's daughter?    Say!

### GAWAIN.

Ne'er spake a purer soul from fairer features ;
And ev'n if outward semblance might deceive,
Her eye, as the blue flame reveals the treasure,
Shows her soul's worth !

### TRISTAN.

          Like down upon the peach
One sees timidity enwrap her being,
And on her brow a child's simplicity.

### PERCIVAL.

You see now, Sirs, that I no braggart am ;
My wife is fair, and that she's more than fair,
That I not thoughtlessly this strife began,
That shall you witness, that shall you announce !
The victory is mine, the Queen must kneel !

### GAWAIN.

Griselda loves her child ; she will refuse him !

### PERCIVAL (*springing up*).

You're dreaming, Sir !    Refuse, to me refuse him !

Sever this right arm if I conquer not.
I was as certain ere my word was given,
As certain, by my beard, as if a contract
Lay signed and sealed already in my hand.
For me she left her father, left her mother,
To me she clung when in her deepest grief;
The victory is mine; the Queen must kneel!

### TRISTAN.

And such a wife, already proved by sorrow,
This strong, this true, this pure, this childlike wife,
You will torment, will torture unto death;
Will with a dagger measure the heart's depths
That only beats for you; with tears will fill
The eye that beams with love in seeking yours!
O do it not!   Repent thee of the thought!

### PERCIVAL.

St. David!   Sir, persistence is my wont,
And never was I more resolved than now
When this contention stimulates my will,
Kindles my blood, on tension puts my heart,
And chases from my soul discouragement,
As from the valleys  wind the mist disperses.
By heavens, this very night shall she be tested!
The victory is mine; the Queen must kneel.

### TRISTAN.

Nay, not to-night!   Disturb her slumber not,
Turn not to gall her joy in your return!
You wound her doubly, wound you her to-night.

### PERCIVAL.

And if I wound her, will the smart remain?
Pain only dreamed of gives a joyful waking.
If a caprice, a simple fancy prompts me
My body to chastise by vigorous fast,
With scourge to rend the flesh from off my back,
Or with my dagger scratch and notch my hand,
Who has the right to blame me?   But Griselda
Is my own wife, flesh is she of my flesh,
Bone of my bone.   Let me but have my way;
You say she loves me: let her prove it, then!

### TRISTAN.

The deed is yours, but mine was counsel true.

### PERCIVAL.

The thought of victory charms me!   And, by heaven,
This night, this moment I will win it!   Here
I'll sit and weave such lines into my face,
And with such wrinkles make my brow to frown,

3*

That not a storm-cloud on tempestuous night
Shall darker threaten than my countenance ;
Nor storm and wind can sigh as I will sigh.
And just in time, Sir Gawain, I bethink me ;
Beneath these heights, within a lowly hut,
Dwells a poor woman who was once my nurse ;
Carry the boy there when Griselda yields him—
But hush, she comes !

### TRISTAN.

Yet once more, Percival !

### PERCIVAL.

Away with words !   And now, as earnest judges,
Prepare to view the contest and the triumph.

---

SCENE IV.—GRISELDA *enters, followed by servants with
tankards and goblets.*

### GRISELDA.

Food is preparing and will soon be ready ;
Meanwhile refresh yourselves, my honored guests,
With brimming goblets of this noble wine.
I drink to you, pledge me in friendly wishes !

### GAWAIN.

Thanks, lady, thanks !   Your welfare in this cup !

### TRISTAN.

I drink to fleeting pain, and lasting joy !

### GRISELDA.

You entered just in time t' escape the tempest
That rages now in fury 'mid the mountains,
With voice of thunder it awakes the echoes,
And flash on flash despatches through the air.

### GAWAIN.

For your defence an angel watches there.

### GRISELDA.

You are too gracious, Sir !
  [*The servants have withdrawn ;* GRISELDA *ap-
   proaches* PERCIVAL, *who, like one overwhelm-
   ed with anxiety, has thrown himself into an
   arm-chair.*
      What, Percival !
You will not drink ?   Refreshment you disdain,
Such as you ever craved ?   What ails you, Sir ?
A veil of anxious thought obscures your features,

And smothered fire flames in your countenance!
Where are the smiles with which you greeted me?
You sigh? Why, Percival! you make me tremble!
What ails you, Sir?

PERCIVAL.

Mere weariness, no more!

GRISELDA.

Not so! Deceive me not! Such gloomy shadows
Did discontent ne'er weave upon thy brow.
What ails thee, Percival? Quick, let me know it!

PERCIVAL.

No! Not to-night! I'll spare you till the morrow!

GRISELDA.

Oh, tell me now whatever I must hear!
Through the long, silent night, let me not watch,
Trembling and troubled, overcome with fear!

PERCIVAL.

Thou choosest, hear it then. The King is angered
That I have grafted on the royal oak
A little willow-twig, and that my son,

Whose heritage will be my sovereignty,
Sprang from the bosom of a collier's child.
And this is his command, that we deliver
Our child into his hands, and that at once ;
If I refuse, he threatens banishment.

GRISELDA (*smiling, after a pause*).

Thou jestest, Percival, thou wilt delude me !
Thou are but trifling with me ; in my face
Thou canst not look unmoved and steadfastly ;
Try if thou canst !   Thou dost evade mine eye,
And thy lip trembles !   Ay, thou smilest now !
Go ! try some other sport, you can't affright me !

PERCIVAL.

'Tis thou who art deceived.   My word is truth,
And these (*pointing to* TRISTAN *and* GAWAIN) are
     bearers of the royal will
And the executors of its command.

GRISELDA.

You too would take my child away from me !
Ah, go, disguise yourselves, that one may fear you !
Slave Rupert clinks his chains when he approaches,
The were-wolf howls when on the track of children !

Ah, gentlemen, you must not play the goblin
In knightly guise, with spurs upon your heels !

### PERCIVAL.

My word thou doubtest, and a thoughtless child
Thou sportest, smiling, with the Terrible ;
Speak you, then, you, the royal messengers,
And be my witnesses.

### TRISTAN.

Sir Percival
Speaks truth.

### GAWAIN.

Truly !   So is it as he says !
We were sent here to take away your child.

### GRISELDA.

It is no jest—the King will tear my child,
My darling child will tear from out my heart ?
But wherefore ?   Why ?   What, shall he penance do
Because his mother's lot was lowliness ?

### PERCIVAL.

He is the King, and royal power is his ;
No opposition to his will he suffers ;
Make thy resolve, deliver up the child.

## GRISELDA.

Thou wert resolvéd, Percival, thou wouldst—
Thou canst a moment think of yielding him?
Thou wilt no longer look upon the features
So full of smiling, full of careless trust?
No more the ring of that sweet voice wilt hear,
When lovingly it cries, " Dear little father?"
O, Percival, thou wilt disown thy child?
Bethink thee of the day on which I bore him,
When thou didst clasp him to thy father's breast,
Crying aloud, "A boy, it is a boy !"
Think of the lively tumult of thy joy;
For him thou didst forget me; from his face
There sprang for thee a living fount of bliss,
There was no star that seemed too far away,
With light and glory to adorn his life,
And now thou giv'st him up? I'll not believe it !
Who can despoil the lion of his young;
No, Percival will not give up his child !

## PERCIVAL.

I must ! Where'er I turn and look for refuge,
I no evasion, no escape can find;
I am constrained this path alone to choose;
'Tis the King's will, I must give up the boy.

### GRISELDA.

Thou hast slain Cathmor, and thou Swen hast slain;
He who slew kings, their anger can sustain:
My Percival, thou'lt not give up the boy!
With every sacrifice that can be made,
Appease our monarch; give him blood and life;
Thy child, thine only child, thou canst not give.

### PERCIVAL.

I tell thee, wife, I must! Thou pleadest vainly!
I must give up the boy! I must and will!

### GRISELDA.

He is my child, as thine he is, I'll see
If thou wilt give him up. He is my blood,
I bore him in my bosom, gave him birth,
I suckled him; it was mine eye that watched
With silent joy his progress beautiful,
And my whole future rests upon his head!
Dare strange caprices tear away my child,
And rob it of the guardianship of love?
        [*She suddenly stops; then goes on in restless haste.*
The King no right possesses to my boy;
He knows him not; his birth has angered him;
He hates him cordially, and when he has him—

Say, gentlemen, what will he with the boy?
What, silent! Say! What will he with the child?

### TRISTAN.

Be not concerned! The King is just and mild.

### GAWAIN.

What was commanded that must be fulfilled;
He gave us orders, but concealed his will.

GRISELDA (*with an expression of utmost anguish.*)

Nay, you deceive me not! It is inscribed
Upon your brows, in your uneasy glances:
He wants to kill him!—Will he? Yes, he will!
For this you'll take from me my darling child,
From me, his mother? Rather both mine eyes!
Attempt it, bloody murderers: come on,
Snatch him if possible from his sweet dreams
Before you see me lifeless at your feet!
Shed, if you can, his blood, ere mine flows forth!
Forsaken child, thy father shields thee not,
I'll do it, I a woman, yet a mother!

GAWAIN (*to* TRISTAN.)

Right well I knew she'd not give up the boy.

PERCIVAL.

Now or never!

(*Turning to* GRISELDA.)

Be it so, Griselda!
Keep thy child, then!   But guard his precious life
Henceforth with sleepless care and vigilance ;
Protect him ever from a breath of air ;
Like a rare gem preserve him, like a crown ;
For thou a costly price for him hast given,
And with the father's life hast bought the boy !

GRISELDA (*with a cry.*)

With thy life, Percival ?

PERCIVAL.

Why tremblest thou ?
Thy precious child remains !   Though I'm proscribed
And made an outlaw, though my power is crushed,
Though through these valleys royal rage pursues me
As he unwearied hunts the timid deer ;
Though treason hastens after, might o'erwhelms,
Although the hangman to the scaffold drags,
Yet hesitate, yet falter not, Griselda !
Leave me unburied, leave my bones to bleach,
Saving thy boy, thy highest wish thou'lt reach !

GRISELDA (*with her folded hands pressed on her heart, looks absently before her for some moments ; then speaks slowly and wearily*).

Does the King's anger threaten banishment,
And put thy life in danger?

PERCIVAL.
Ay, Griselda!

GRISELDA (*almost inaudibly*).
Then take away the boy!

PERCIVAL.
Thou wilt contend
No more; thou giv'st the child?

GRISELDA.
I must!!!—

PERCIVAL.
The victory's mine! Sir Gawain, take the boy!
[GAWAIN *approaches the next room*, GRISELDA *hastens after him.*

GRISELDA.
Hold! Take him! Stay! I cannot, God in heaven!

PERCIVAL.

Hither, my Griselda !

> [GRISELDA *turns, throws herself at* PERCIVAL'S *feet, and looks up to him with her clasped hands on his knees. As* GAWAIN *enters the ante-room the curtain falls.*

# THIRD ACT.

SCENE I.— *Castle Pendennys—A richly-adorned saloon.*

PERCIVAL (*springing up*).

If right it is or wrong?   That is the question!
But mine own right to use, cannot be wrong;
Yet what I dare, I should do joyfully;
I am not joyful, wherefore am I not?

> [*He walks up and down restlessly; standing still
> again, he proceeds:*

That which torments me is a mere chimera!
I through so many charming days have yearned,
Yea, felt constrained to know, not to believe,
With mine own eye to see, with mine own ear
To hear, and tangibly with mine own hand
To seize upon and hold conviction fast;
For there is faith in all things, e'en in madness!
But I for proofs have longed, and I have sighed
For one of the first tests of destiny;
And shall I tremble now at their mere aspect,
And from their phantoms shrink?

(69)

I prove my war-horse ere in him I trust ;
I prove my armor's weight, and my sword's temper,
Before the noise of battle rages round me ;
And may not prove my wife ?

     Shall I, for a mere fancy, lose the pleasure
Of looking down into her inmost soul,
To see mine image in its crystal mirror,
Mine image only, none approaching it,
To see her spirit so to mine enthralled,
By my breath ruffled, trembling at my look.
Moved by the slightest motion of my brows,
That in my will she feels and she exists,
That I am all in all to her on earth :
Her lord, her king, her destiny, her god !
Love knows no line or measure, knows no bound,
No more, no less, is indivisible,
And if one grain is wanting in its weight,
A mote, an atom, then it is not love !
And shall I bind me to the possible,
When a mere test authenticates the real ?
And shall I rest content with empty trust
When I can revel in a certainty ?
Truly what tortures me is a chimera !

SCENE II.—PERCIVAL—GAWAIN—*Later*, TRISTAN.

PERCIVAL (*rushing up to* GAWAIN).

Now, Gawain, say where have you left my boy?

GAWAIN.

In faithful keeping, noble Percival,
Yet hostile is he to attendant strange,
And with his hands with scorn repulses her;
He weeps, and with his father's anger threatens
The hand that tore him from his mother's arms.

PERCIVAL.

He will complain to me, and of myself?
Now, by mine oath he's not so far from right,
And in due time I'll make atonement for it!
But say, Sir Gawain, have you summoned them,
My knights and vassals, unto Pendennys?

GAWAIN.

From all the valleys they are flowing hither.

PERCIVAL.

Thank you!                         [TRISTAN *appears.*
But see, what bring you us, Sir Tristan?
Saw you Griselda?

### TRISTAN.

Yes, I saw her, Sir!

### PERCIVAL.

You found her sorely troubled, and in tears?
You hesitate?   Speak!   You shall naught conceal!

### TRISTAN.

In bearing to Griselda thy command
To meet thee here, I through apartments passed,
Until I reached the turret's winding stair,
That upward leads to the bow-windowed room;
And having reached the door that open stood,
With scope for sight and sound, I saw Griselda.
Her hair fell limp and unadorned about her,
A stony image, motionless she sat,
Scarce breathing, dead though living; on her cheek
Not even the color of a faded rose,
And from her eyes such seas of sorrow fell,
That overflowed by tears, her lips, in truth,
A cup of wormwood drank.   Upon her lap
There lay a plaything that had been her child's;—
Once joy to him, now sting to her distress.
She sat bent over, with her folded hands
Laid passive on her lap, and steadfast looked

On her child's cradle, like to one benumbed.
A sigh, heart-rending, from her tortured breast
Wrung itself sharply out, her briny tears
Gushed forth again redoubled and afresh.
She pressed the toy with ardor to her breast,
And echoed now from heaven and now from earth,
She cried aloud, My child, my darling child !
And crying thus a heart-string broke within
And lifeless sank she down upon the earth !

PERCIVAL.

Enough !   Enough !

TRISTAN.

                    In her attendant's arms,
A dawning life and strength crept slowly back :
She raised herself : a picture caught her eye,
The dolorous mother gazing on her Son ;
Trembling, she staggered toward it, bent the knee ;
Her hands devoutly folded on her breast,
Her quivering lips convulsed and cramped together,
She bowed her head.   The veil of clouds was rent
That lay on hill and mountain dark without,
A ray of sunshine came and kissed her cheek,
And all her features with its light illumed ;

4

She smiled, O Sir, what think you, said the smile?
The bud has fall'n, the flower shall fade erewhile.

[PERCIVAL *looks down in silence ; after a pause,*
　　TRISTAN *steps nearer, and continues.*

That saw I, Sir, and sharing in her grief,
Unmanned by witnessing her martyrdom,
My own eye moistened, hastened I away,
With her attendants leaving thy behest.

PERCIVAL (*after a pause proudly erects himself.*)

Dost thou begin to tremble, Percival?
Is thy strong nature overwhelmed by tears?
The cup is filled and she must empty it;
It is resolved on, it shall be fulfilled!
I will, I must, I have no other path.

TRISTAN.

No other path?　Here lies one close at hand ;
A single word will soothe Griselda's grief;
A single word the clouds will scatter wide,
That fold her spirit in a starless night!
Explain the riddle of this cruel sport,
And to the mother's arms restore her boy.

PERCIVAL.

What of my honor, what my plighted word?

TRISTAN.

Have it redeemed in presence of the Queen.


PERCIVAL.

What, I shall kneel? shall kneel before her feet?


TRISTAN.

Thy pride conceived this outrage; humble it.


PERCIVAL.

I, never! never! Not for all earth's treasures!
Not for a life! Not for a heavenly kingdom!
A woman's tears are like the summer shower,
That sprinkles gently down from fleeting clouds;
It passes over, and the sun bursts forth,
And the well-watered fields grow fresh and green.
Griselda shall make proof what love can do;
But when th' appointed course she shall have run,
When from this night of clouds she has emerged,
I with a rainbow will enarch her sky;
Its thousand hues shall float above her head;
One rapture only all her life shall be!
I much demand and your reproof is vital,
But I, too, am the man to make requital!

### GAWAIN.

Banners are waving yonder on the heights,
And armor glitters in the vale below;
They are your vassals, and assembled, Sir.

### PERCIVAL.

I will go forth to meet th' approaching host;
And you meanwhile, with re-assuring words,
Prepare the tender heart of my Griselda
For this new torture; tell me, will you not?

### GAWAIN.

It shall be done.

### TRISTAN.

     Your wish shall be fulfilled.

### PERCIVAL.

Farewell, then!   Soon the drama will be ended,
Already I rejoice as conqueror.    [*Goes.*

### TRISTAN.

Ay!   But the angel who the record keeps
Of our life's seed-time, unto thee shall mete
A victory that ends in thy defeat.

### GAWAIN.

Here comes Griselda ; slowly through the halls
She by her host of servants is conducted.

### TRISTAN.

The picture she of grief!   Like the full ear,
Her heavy head droops downward to the earth.

---

## SCENE III.

### GRISELDA (*to her women.*)

For all your love accept my warmest thanks!
My steps no longer need to be supported.
I beg you leave me now;  it all is over !
(*The women retire to the background;* GRISELDA *steps
forth.*)
Speak, noble knights, where tarries Percival ?
It was at his request I hither came.

### GAWAIN.

Not long need you await his coming, lady.

### TRISTAN.

You turn away your face from us in anger,
Our very presence with abhorrence fills you;

Just is your hatred, and your just reproach
Though wordless 'tis, speaks loudly to my soul.

### GRISELDA.

Hate you?   Nay, noble knights, I hate you not;
I no man hate, not even the King himself.

### GAWAIN.

And yet his is the hand that wounded you.

### GRISELDA.

The deed was his; the will was from above.
Not his the hand that presses on my head:
Th' Omnipotent of whom the air is full,
Who tosses crowns about like feather-down,
Who knits His brow, and kingdoms shake and fall,
Who nods, and worlds appear, and stars shine forth,
Who nods, and they are gone!   He smote me, He!
God tried the strength of this my haughty heart,
And see, it broke, and into tears dissolved.

### TRISTAN.

So humble, so submissive in your grief!

### GRISELDA.

So humble and submissive?   Was I not
Right full of haughty pride and self-conceit?

Received I not as if they were my due,
The love of Percival, and then his hand?
Was I not proud when I was called his wife?
Did I not glory in my beauteous child?
But I in lowly poverty was born;
Nor recognized the favor shown by heaven,
But took as mine own right its tender gift;
So in my boy the Lord admonished me,
He, blameless, makes atonement for my guilt.


### TRISTAN.

O, guard the pious mind that strengthens you,
With patience clad, with patience arm your soul!
Yet darker is the fate that comes to meet you,
Still greater sacrifice the King requires.


### GRISELDA.

Yet greater sacrifice? Say, what demands he?
Threatens he Percival with his displeasure?
Does he demand my life? Speak! Let me know!


### GAWAIN.

Fear not for Percival! The King's displeasure
Threatens your life!

### GRISELDA.

Make known to me his will!
What he demands, make known!

### GAWAIN.

Then hear : he wills
That Percival the marriage tie unloose
That bound him unto you, and choose a wife
Of noble lineage equal to his own,
To give him heirs befitting to his rank.

### GRISELDA.

O gloomy phantom of my troubled dreams,
So quickly hast thou come!   A single day
From my brow snatches every crown of joy,
And plucks away the only flower of hope!
Husband and child!   Alone, and desolate,
A sea of sorrows gathered in one breast!
And he?   And Percival—O let me know it,
What answered Percival?

### TRISTAN.

His heart was heavy
When he obeyed his master, that his race
Might not prove traceless in the stream of time,
And distant ages still his fame regard.

### GRISELDA.

I have foreseen it! Many a silent night
My spirit prophesied it! Far too rich,
Too perfect was my happiness for life;
It could but hover o'er me as a dream,
And like a lovely dream must flee away.
I see it plainly, it should come to this!
Should he deny himself a father's joys?
And unto strangers alienate his rights?
Who can reproach him? He has rightly done.

### GAWAIN.

Can you conceive it, Tristan? She defends him!

### GRISELDA.

So turn thee home into the forest shadows,
Thou child of poverty and servitude!
Never within this castle was thy place,
Upon its threshold bravely turn thy back;
With thee thou tak'st his image, bear'st thy dreams.
Thou wast by him beloved, and that affection
No royal mandate from his heart can drive;
He will remember thee, will ne'er forget thee,
He feels with thee the sundering of these ties!
O, comfort thee and learn to yield, my heart!

4*

Be strong! No tears shalt thou from him exact,
Nor with complaints add stings to his distress;
But you, most noble knights, make known to me,
Drives me this very day my fate from hence?
Shall I not see him more?

### GAWAIN.

Sir Percival
Himself your sentence will make known to you:
In open hall, before his nobles all,
He will dissolve your union, and your fate
This day restores you to your forest home.

### TRISTAN.

There sound his hasty footsteps in the hall.
Now summon to you all your nature's strength,
And calmly go to meet your cruel lot.

---

SCENE IV.—PERCIVAL *joins the preceding with some of his most renowned vassals; is joined by his remaining Knights and vassals, who enter noiselessly.*

### PERCIVAL (*after a pause.*)

Receive my greetings, vassals, men at arms!
As it beseems, you come in ranks complete

Unto Pendennys, to my feudal halls;
I called you and you came.  If now amazed
And wondering you ask, and cannot guess,
Wherefore I called you, this is my response :
You know how, stimulated by your prayers,
Griselda there I took to be my wife;
Child of the woods, low was her origin,
Though full of graces, virtuous, and true !
You know that she a little son hath borne me,
As heir to my domains you greeted him :
Our royal master and our lord, King Arthur,
Rejecting both my marriage and its fruit,
Demands renunciation of the child,
That the dominion and the dignity
Descending to my race from eagle proud,
Be not degraded to a sparrow's brood ;
And truly I the King's behest fulfil.

> [GRISELDA *shrinks painfully into herself ;*
> *after a pause* PERCIVAL *proceeds.*

To the King's messengers the child I gave.
Yet farther still, my royal master wills
That I his sister, Morgana, should wed,
Griselda there from out my castle thrusting,
In open hall, before my noble men,
As in their sight I took her for my wife.

And in obedience to the King's command,
I in this open hall assemble you,
To see me yield myself to his behest.

#### ONE OF PERCIVAL'S KNIGHTS.

What, Percival?

#### ANOTHER.

Thou hast decided, Sir?

#### A THIRD.

Thou wilt disown thy wife, disown Griselda?

#### PERCIVAL.

Be silent there!   Silenced by my displeasure!
You are called hither but as witnesses,
And not to sit in judgment on my deeds.
Behold and listen then, but tame your tongues!
Step forth, Griselda!

#### GRISELDA.

Here I am, my lord!

#### PERCIVAL.

Listen and understand!   The sacred ties
That once united us, now  severed are :

This hour our mutual compact renders void !
Griselda, dost thou hear ?

### GRISELDA.

I do, my lord !

### PERCIVAL.

This very day depart thou from these halls.
And all the gifts with which my love endow'd thee,
Thy garments, jewels, all embellishments,
That do but heighten charms they cannot give,
Leave these behind ; for so decrees the King :
That thou shalt leave me helpless, naked, poor,
As naked, poor and helpless I received thee ;
And thus, before the King's ambassadors,
And the executors of his command,
Dismiss I thee.    Depart !

### GRISELDA.

My honored lord,
When from my lowly hut thou brought'st me home
To this proud castle, to unite thy power,
Thy name, thy dignity to nothingness,
O'erwhelmed with love the charcoal-burner's child,
When my felicity bloomed forth apace

Like flowers that open in a single night;
A voice spake warning in my inmost soul :
Thy happiness shall not outlive the flowers,
And as it bloomed shall fade within a night.
And yielding to the dictate of my fate,
Not as a gift did I receive thy troth,
But as a loan, with love for interest,
Lightly recalled as it was lightly given.
And since thou now announcest that the day
Of reckoning has come, I'll not delay.
Take back what from thy hand I have received,
The proud adornment of nobility,
The clang of name, prëeminence, and pomp
With which thy lavish hand invested me.
Yet lingering only, with a heart oppressed,
I give thee back the best and costliest
Of all the gifts thy love on me conferred;
Receive this ring, of love the sign and pledge,
That made us one, and blessed in making one;
It was my all, receive it back ! And so—
So go I helpless, poor, and naked hence,
As helpless, poor, and naked hither came I.

PERCIVAL.

What thou hast brought with thee that take away,
Not more, not less.

GRISELDA.

Full well, thou knowest, Sir,
How thou didst bear me from my father's house;
An apron and a wretched woolen dress
I brought to thee.   No beast of burden needs
To bear my scanty goods from hence away.

PERCIVAL.

Then take thine apron and thy woolen dress.

GRISELDA.

So will I, Sir!   What else was once mine own,
When for the castle I exchanged the hut,
Youth's cheerful heart, the bloom of innocence,
The spirit full of trust and full of hope,
These gifts I bartered for yet sweeter joys,
And for the memories of a happy past;
In one thing only thou my debtor art,
For, leaving thee, my love remains behind,
As of thy ring my hand the trace retains,
So thy belovéd image will my soul.

PERCIVAL.

A pointed arrow is her every word,
And every look a double-edgéd sword!
Hasten, Griselda, for thy time is past!

### One of Percival's Knights.

How discontent and pity rend my heart!

### Another.

O that obedience my lips should seal!

### Griselda.

A single word yet trembles on my lips,
Then turning from this castle I will fly
To the maternal bosom of the wilds.
Farewell, my Percival! This loving heart
Will ne'er forget the bliss endowed by thee.
'Twill think of thee when my remembrance long
In these apartments has for aye grown dim;
For the dead past is like a withered leaf,
Swept lightly by, amid the whirl of time.
But henceforth live thou only joyful days!
Surrounded by the choicest gifts of heaven,
Thine ancient trunk keep green with noble shoots;
May laurel wreaths and crowns thee overwhelm,
And wife yet more beloved supply my place;
O I will smile, will smile amid my tears,
If happier she makes thee; love thee more
Can no one, no one on the whole round globe.

PERCIVAL (*milder, and with difficulty concealing his emotion*).

Depart, Griselda, for thy time is past!

### GRISELDA.

I stretch my arms out for a last embrace,
But they are empty; and mine eye seeks thine,
And thou thy face concealest from my sight!
Yes, thou art right; wherefore augment my grief,
And push it to the horrors of despair?
We must be parted, quickly be it done!
Farewell, my Percival!  With this one word
I put the cup of sorrow to my lips
And drink it dry; for this one bitter word
Says all things, Percival!  The lexicon
Of grief has only this one word: Farewell!
Farewell, my Percival!

### PERCIVAL.
Depart, Griselda!

GRISELDA (*with a glance towards heaven*).

The Lord commandeth, and the maid obeys.
[*She turns towards the background;* PERCIVAL
*deeply moved, covers his face, while the women
of* GRISELDA *press about her, weeping.*

### One of the Women.

Say, dost thou leave us ?

### Another.

Wilt thou leave us, lady ?

### A Third.

Permit me first thy garment's hem to kiss !

### Griselda.

Leave me : my time is past, I must away !

### One of Percival's Knights.

Farewell, Griselda !

### Another.

God go with you, lady !

### Griselda.

Farewell to all !   Though driven hence by fate,
One comfort yet is left me in my pain ;
I go lamenting, but I go lamented !

> [*She passes through the crowd that accompanies her*
> *in great agitation.* Percival *looks after her*
> *till she has left the hall, then rushes down from*
> *the estrade, seizes* Tristan *by the hand, and*
> *leads him hastily forward some steps.*

PERCIVAL.

Tristan!   I was too harsh!   By all in heaven!
'Twas not well done.

TRISTAN.

   Thou followedst blindly
The counsel of thine own proud heart; 'tis done.
The deed was thine; endure its anguish now!

PERCIVAL.

I was too harsh; her love with grief requited,
And of her soul the harmony transformed
Into rude discord!
     [*Sound of trumpets heard.*
   Hark, the clang of horns;
Who greets, with cheers of joy, this evil house?

GAWAIN (*at the window*).

See!   Troops of servants in tumultuous crowds
Fill up the castle's court; a cavalcade
Is passing 'neath the gateway's groaning arch,
And England's colors float upon the breeze!
Here comes Ginevra, by her court attended,
And Lancelot is present in the throng

#### PERCIVAL.

O that a thunder-storm would drive them homeward
Whence they came hither !

#### TRISTAN (*steps to the window*).

Ay, it is the Queen !
Sir Lancelot has helped her to dismount :
Supported by his arm she nears the hall.
Whence borne along by the surrounding crowd,
Griselda, in departing, goes to meet her.

#### PERCIVAL.

Griselda, say you ?

#### TRISTAN.

Yes, I say Griselda !
See, she looks up, and doth behold the Queen,
And deep the color glows upon her cheek !
She presses to the wall, and bows the knee,
Yet Queen Ginevra passes proudly by,
Scarce condescending on thy wife to look,
Who now, once more urged forward by the throng,
Her weary steps toward the gate directs.

#### GAWAIN.

Sir Percival ! Behold here comes the Queen !

SCENE V.—*Enter* QUEEN GINEVRA, *attended by* LANCE-
LOT, ORIANA, *and other Knights and Ladies*—PERCIVAL
*goes to meet them with* TRISTAN *and* GAWAIN.

### GINEVRA.

We fear that we as not too welcome guests
Enter this castle, noble Percival;
For undecided in the air is poised
Our contest still; yet we deceive ourselves,
If in a guest thou seest an enemy,
And fail'st to give us hospitable shelter,
When we the King's approach to you announce;
The hunt has drawn him into Stafford's woods,
And food and lodging here he hopes to find.

### PERCIVAL.

Not his own house shall greet him with such joy
As that with which Pendennys welcomes him.

### GINEVRA.

We thank you for your courteous reception!
And now permit us, Percival, to ask:
What means the throng that met us at your gates,
And what the multitude of mingled tones

Resounding in our ears?   Is it a feast
You are about to give?   Or held you court?
Who was the woman by the crowd surrounded,
Who met us at the entrance of the hall?

### PERCIVAL.

It was Griselda, Queen, it was my wife,
From whose maternal breast I tore her child,
It was my wife, whom I disgraced, disowned.

### GINEVRA.

Griselda, say you?

### ORIANA.

What, she gave her child?

### TRISTAN.

With burning tears, but with a steadfast heart,
For Percival she made the sacrifice.

### LANCELOT.

She gave her child?   She went from Pendennys?
Willingly, say you, unresisting went?

### TRISTAN.

Bewept and weeping from Pendennys halls
To the mean hovel of the woods she passed,

No angry word escapéd from her lips,
And blessings were her parting salutation.

### GAWAIN.

'Twas even so, as I can testify,
But understand it, that I cannot do.

### PERCIVAL.

Ay, Queen, so is it! If on this rude earth,
One of God's angels visibly appeared,
Reaping for love a harvest of fell hate,
For benedictions curses, 'tis Griselda,
Ay, my Griselda, and the collier's child!
My reckless word I have redeemed, Ginevra;
It is enough! Let wicked mummery
No more profane the heaven of her breast;
Grief shall no longer gnaw upon her heart,
Her worth has been made known, let us revere it.

### LANCELOT.

So be it, Queen! Away with pique and rancor,
With claims contending, enmity and strife.
Let words atone for what mere words have done.

### GINEVRA.

Sir Lancelot, when counsel we desire,
Doubt not we shall a consultation call!

But you, however, Percival, astound us.
Is this the man who in his haughty pride
The collier's child exalted over us,
Who as a paragon paraded her,
And of her virtues did so vaunt himself?
Two garlands ostentatious crown thy brow,
Dost thou shrink back in terror from the third?
What strange delusion blinds your senses, say,
That thus from victory you turn away?


### PERCIVAL.

What!   Of her tears lies there not weight enough
Upon my soul, called I not pain enough
Upon her sinless, consecrated head?
It is enough!   I tell you in plain words:
I know what I resolved and what I did,
Not a step farther will I in this course!


### GINEVRA.

This was my stipulation; you assenting:
Though to its very depths her soul was pierced,
Griselda should maintain for you her favor,
The glow of love to hatred not be turned,
Nor heavenly patience into bitterness;

In her affront cling closer to your side
Than when you first embraced her as your bride.
Was not this my condition ?   You who heard me,
Spake I not thus ?

### GAWAIN.

So spakest thou, my Queen !

### ORIANA.

I heard it also ; thus it was agreed.

### GINEVRA.

We doubt not that Griselda's lofty soul
Amid its sorrows clung in love to you ;
You lack not will, nor I in faith am weak ;
There's but a trifle wanting : 'tis the proof.
You see a final struggle still awaits you ;
But to attempt it I will not constrain you,
For if repentance seize you, or if pity
Should overthrow the pride that reigns within,
Sir Percival, you can do penance meet,
And make atonement kneeling at my feet !

### PERCIVAL.

I shall kneel, I ?

5

ORIANA.

Sir Percival, declare ;
You entered on this contest joyfully,
What apprehension blanches now your cheek ?
You must have fancied, Sir, that she would smile
When you should tear her child from out her arms,
And when you from your castle thrust her out,
She would depart as calm and satisfied
As if she merely went to see a neighbor.


PERCIVAL (*aside*).

Oh, if I fancied so, my only crime
Would be but downright imbecility ;
But in the distance I foresaw her tears,
And counted every sigh that rent her heart.


ORIANA.

And on reflection, Sir, what do they prove,
The trials that Griselda overcame ?
She gave her child that else were torn from her,
And hence she went but to avoid constraint ;
The one true test, I think, is yet to come.
Griselda's worth will only be obscured
If you forestall and paralyze compassion ;
It lies too near to be by flight evaded.

### PERCIVAL.

Ruinous net which I myself have spun !
I must fulfil that which I have begun.


### GINEVRA.

Choose, Percival, and so redeem your word !
Either to kneel, as vanquished, at my feet,
Or go at once to seek Griselda out.
A banished fugitive, crave her protection ;
And if she grants it, if the wife disowned
Defies for you the power that threatens her,
Will venture head and life, and all for you,
Then be the victor, and the sooty maid
Sees England's Queen low kneeling at her feet.


### TRISTAN.

Nay, gracious Queen, the bow-string do not stretch
Unto the very limits of its strength !
And thou, thou yet dost linger, Percival !
Dost not turn shuddering back ?   Oh, ask thine heart !
Within thine hands thou holdest weal and woe !
Thou holdest pride or love, hold'st life or death !
And thou canst linger ?   Hast a right to choose ?
Kneel, Percival, 'tis for Griselda, kneel !

LANCELOT (*to* GINEVRA).

Prolong not thus th' endurance of her pain,
Ginevra !   Let Griselda's sufferings move thee.


GINEVRA.

Griselda's fate is lying in his hands ;
He can to conflict, can to peace direct it !
Decide, Sir Percival.


ORIANA.

                       Why hesitate ?
Obey the impulse of your better nature !
Down on your knees, ask pardon, do not fear
Perchance those tender knees to wound in bending ;
Thou upon down shalt kneel, on eider-down !
'Tis easier than you think, to make atonement !
No eye will see it !   We will silence keep,
To the best friend hardly confiding it,
That Percival has knelt before Ginevra.


PERCIVAL (*looks gloomily before him ; after a pause :*)

I have done outrage to the noblest heart,
Have revelled in her death-like agony ;
And, recognizing now my dreadful guilt,
How gladly would I now her head defend

From what my duty calls on me to end!
But now it is too late!   I'll fill my measure!
I am prepared a contest new to make,
And it to-day, this moment undertake.


### GINEVRA.

Proceed, then!   Nor will we remain behind.
Attend us, gentlemen; and soon we'll see
Whose scale will fall, whose the ascendant be.
     [*Away with* ORIANA, PERCIVAL, LANCELOT, GA-
     WAIN, *and their roving followers.*


### TRISTAN.

Fly hence, unhappy one!   The hardest lot
That love may fall on has befallen thee!
By the same lip thou'rt deified and scorned,
By the same hand thou art caressed and stabbed!

# FOURTH ACT.

*Forest among the mountains—A cascade, near which, surrounded by trees, stands the collier's hut.*

SCENE I.—*Old* CEDRIC *appears, led by a* BOY.

CEDRIC.

Can I believe thee, boy? Heardst thou it rightly?
Her child she has delivered to the King?

BOY.

So said I.

CEDRIC.

And her sacred marriage tie
Is by the King's command made null and void?

BOY.

It is, blind Cedric, yes!

CEDRIC.

And she disowned
In open hall, in presence of the knights?

(102)

BOY.

Just as I told it thee, so was the thing;
And all who hear it Percival condemn,
And the King with them.

CEDRIC.

                    Words!   Mere empty sounds!
The Count of Wales paraded pompously,
His haughty head far reaching to the clouds,
And words, and words!   Until the breath of curses
Reaches such heights as those, soft flattery
Will into fragrance change its pois'nous breath,
And out of imprecations balsam charm!
A collier's daughter and the Count of Wales!
Master and servant!   Yet they both were made
Of the same dust, both Count and collier, children
Of the one God who dwells in heaven above!
What heardest thou beside?

BOY.

                    Where'er I went
I heard the mournful voice of lamentation;
The poor were weeping; for their kind physician,
Yearning I heard the sick and feeble cry,

From every tongue Griselda's praises rang,
With testimonials that she undeserved
Was reaping sorrow where she blessings sowed !


### CEDRIC.

We mortals judge by merest empty show ;
But God's eye plunges to our very depths !
Gentle may be the hand, and gifts dispense,
May clothe the naked, and may nurse the sick ;
But when within a heart pride makes its nest,
When haughtiness with piety parades,
Not undeserved is heaven's thunderbolt.


### BOY.

What !   Speakest thus of thine own flesh and blood ?


### CEDRIC.

I cut my hand off if it angers me,
And if my blood runs madly through my veins,
A vein I open till it flows aright.
O there is evil, black-fermented blood !
Enough !   Thou art too young for things like these !
Come, boy, conduct me to the mossy seat
Beneath the oak-tree yonder !

BOY.

Here, blind Cedric!
Here sit and take your rest!


CEDRIC (*sinking down upon the moss*).

O, flight of time!
Sighing, my memory follows after her!
Here sat she often in the twilight dim,
Close by my side, or coaxingly she crept
Into my arms, and chatted with me there,
And sang—thou know'st the song—come, sing it, boy!
How did it run?  A knight there was—No, thus,—


> The gallant knight was riding by,
>     A little rose he chanced to see ;
> And as its beauty caught his eye,
>     He wished his own the rose to be.


So ran it!  Sing to me that song!  Nay, sing not!
Sing it not, boy!  It is a hateful song!
A song that sickens me!  I will not hear
How the knight stole my rose away from me.


BOY.

Come to your house now, Cedric, you need rest!
5*

CEDRIC.

I would have borne it bravely had she died;
I should have been alone, but not forsaken,
Truly unloved, yet by my child denied not;
And bore I all the sorrows in the world
Upon these shoulders, one I should not bear;
My child would have relieved me of the worst,
But with her base ingratitude I'm cursed!
Who comes there? Hark!

BOY.

The wind but stirs the leaves.

CEDRIC.

Nay, footsteps are they, footsteps! They come nearer!
'Twere an ill moment for her, came she now!

BOY.

Just at the forest edge a woman passed.

---

SCENE II.—GRISELDA *appears in the background.*

CEDRIC.

Dost know her, boy? Speak, do not hesitate!

#### Boy.

Here is she, speak to her!

#### Cedric.

Who art thou? Speak!

#### Griselda (*sinking at his feet.*)

Thy child, my father, thy forsaken child!

#### Cedric.

My child? Have I a child? Ay, tell me boy:
Have I a child? My heart knows naught of children,
And by my memory I am written childless!

#### Boy.

Pass thy hand o'er her features, know her, Cedric!
It is thy child! Griselda speaks to thee!

#### Cedric (*touching* Griselda's *garment.*)

You are Griselda, wife of Percival?
Ah, fairest lady, let me kiss your hand!
You wear a woolen dress, and wear an apron,
Not gauzy textures, neither silken garments!
Beseems so little pomp your dignity?

Where have you left your ladies and your knights?
Where are your servants?   Ho!   Bring matting here,
Lest morning-dews my lady's feet should wet.

### GRISELDA.

Forsaken, banished, lie I at thy feet,
Thrust from my husband's bed and from his house,
Robbed of the child, the offspring of our love!
Pour not contempt and scorn into my wounds,
Master and father, thou dost rend my heart!

### CEDRIC.

Yes, charming words come flowing from thy mouth;
Upon an anvil forgéd was thy heart,
And seven times hardened was it into steel:
Thy false, deceitful, and ungrateful heart.

### GRISELDA.

Now by His name who sits above the clouds,
Thou dost accuse me of a crime I know not!
Perfidious and ungrateful am I not.

### CEDRIC.

Thou knowest not thy crime, and shakest off
Reproof as lightly as thou wouldst a rain-drop!
Now, then, come give a reckoning of thy love,

Thy truth and thy devotion unto me.
What didst thou, say, thou child affectionate,
When Percival from out his castle drove me,
Because when I the innocent defended,
My interference roused his pride and rage,
For thy blind father, say, what didst thou then?

#### GRISELDA.

I wept, my father!

#### CEDRIC.

                  Are thy tears, then, pearls
That thou shouldst rate them higher than the word,
The frank and earnest word with which the daughter,
With which the house-wife should oppose her husband,
When she her injured father should defend?

#### GRISELDA.

Let not thy child her husband's faults atone;
He was the master, him I must obey.

#### CEDRIC.

Obedience, yes! But silence, silence not!
Not as a husband dost thou honor him,
Not as thy lord, and father of thy child;

But thou idolater to him hast been :
With halos and with clouds of light surrounded,
Saw'st thou a mortal man, a child of dust.
O simpleton, to fling thyself so low
For rank and power to trample under feet;
O slavish meekness, that thy flesh and blood
Could so disown ; receive thy wages now.
His wife thou wast not, thou wert but his wench,
And therefore he disowned thee like a maid.

### GRISELDA.

Angel of God, look down on me from heaven,
And see, and see th' injustice I endure !
Was 't not enough of every joy to rob me ?
Why on my guiltless head must curses fall ?

### CEDRIC.

Thou askest wherefore ? Listen, I will tell thee.
Three days she lay, thy mother and my wife,
Three days lay prostrate, and she could not die,
For yearnings for the child so fondly loved,
Fastened with chains her spirit unto life.
Her latest breath called blessings on thy head ;
Yet cam'st thou not the blessing to receive,
So Satan, lurking near, it would not leave

Upon her dying lips, but stole it thence,
And in his hand he did it so condense,
That upon thee a thunderbolt he hurled it,
Curse of ingratitude, and curse of pride.

### GRISELDA.

I call the eternal God to be my witness,
That base ingratitude was never mine;
Well knows He what I suffered, when my mother
Lay on her death-bed, Percival on his;
When in my husband's death-pangs I was needed,
My mother in her death-pangs for me pleaded.
But yet my marriage-vow was unto him;
I must fulfil the vow I made to him;
Till I had saved the father for the child,
I durst not venture to my mother's bed.

### CEDRIC.

Thou speakest of my grandson, of thy child;
Say, didst thou guard it as a mother should?
As guarded thee thy mother?   Hast thou loved him?
With thy life's blood hast thou defended him?
Thou hast betrayed thy child, ay, thou hast sold him,
To the King's hangman hast delivered him!
The savage beast gives battle for his young,

And even while the fox a hen is strangling,
She drives away her brood !   But thou, but thou !
Thou wast not of a single hair despoiled ;
Of thy gay garment not a fold was wrinkled ;
Thou gav'st him painless up, ay, gave him smiling !

### GRISELDA.

Love gave him me, and love returnéd him.
The husband's life, the father's was in question,
How could I hesitate and how resist ?

### CEDRIC.

Enough of words !   Enough of empty clangor !
For Percival and for his titled name,
Forgot was filial duty, love maternal,
And thy blind father's insult was ignored.
But God is just; and by His will elected,
He once thine idol, now becomes thy scourge,
Hanging thy future fate on my compassion,
Whom in prosperity thou didst forget.

### GRISELDA.
My father, hear me !

### CEDRIC.
                    Nay, I will not hear !
Come, boy, come hither, guide me to my hut,

And mark my word !   The shelter of my house
Denied I never to the fugitive :
To thee I give it also !   There's the threshold ;
The door is open, but my arms are not !
I'll give thee shelter, feed thee, keep from harm ;
But thou shalt not support me with thine arm,
No more shall read my soul  thine eye defiled ;
Thou art my guest, and thou hast been my child !

GRISELDA.

My father, hear me !

CEDRIC.

         Nay, I'll nothing hear !
The deed has spoken, words can not delude me !

        *[He goes off, led by the boy.*

GRISELDA.

So hear you me, then, you, the clouds of heaven,
And thou all-seeing golden sunbeam, hear,
Thou eye of God look down, look down on me !
Thou milder Father in that light enthroned,
Thou know'st my heart, and thou hast proved my soul !
The grief that rent my breast was seen by Thee,
When nigh to death I knew my mother lay,
And him before mine eyes I dying saw.

Not sinful pride infected my weak heart,
Nor was my mind by outward show perverted ;
Lord, if for guilt I suffer, make it known,
What men transgression call, was love alone,
And crime it was not, never, never crime !

     *[After a pause, with quiet composure :*
The joyful spring-time of my life departed,
And sank the bright sun of my happiness ;
The darkness of the night would now enfold me,
And still the star of love has not yet set ;
They unclasped hands, but tore not heart from heart.
The tears that now are glowing on my cheek
Hold kinship with the tears that glow on his.
The sighs that breathe from out this aching breast
Meet his in the vast ocean of the air !
Up !   Arm thyself with courage, humbled soul !
Yield not thyself to dark and painful dreams ;
Thou art not wretched, for thou art beloved !
Chained in thy bosom's depths, compose thy grief,
And if it, swelling, would o'erleap its bounds,
And urge thy lips to utter its sad sounds,
Remember, thou'rt beloved, mayst dare to love,
And upwards, upwards ever raise thine eye !

   *[She sinks exhausted upon the mossy seat ; after a*
     *short pause,* PERCIVAL *and* GAWAIN *appear*
     *in the background.*

## SCENE III.—GRISELDA, PERCIVAL, GAWAIN.

### PERCIVAL.

Alas, that to this strife my word constrains me.
That in the selfish longing of my soul
To revel in the fulness of her love,
I sacrificed her peace and with it mine!
But for this wild delusion of my brain
I would say: No, and dare all England's scorn!
We near the end.   Does the Queen follow us?

### GAWAIN.

She waits our signal in the thicket yonder,
And there amid the foliage rests Griselda!

### PERCIVAL.

'Tis she!   Away, among the bushes hide you;
I'll keep my word and thou shalt witness it.

[GAWAIN goes.

GRISELDA (*deep in thought, speaks half aloud.*)
Thus spake the knight unto the rose,

> Why wither in this forest's night?
> My hat thy beauty should adorn
> With all its blushes bright,
> Not on thy hat will I be worn,
> But worn upon thy heart.

[She sees PERCIVAL.

Ah, Percival!

PERCIVAL.

'Tis I! Dost fly from me?

GRISELDA.

'Tis thou! ah, yes, 'tis thou! Thou standest living,
In blooming, bright reality before me;
No phantom pale of memory, dost thou
Emerge from out the fantasies of dreams.
'Tis really thou, and from thy lips proceeds
The sound of words, thy heart pulsates with life,
Deep glows thine eye, and ruddy is thy cheek,
Within these arms I can encircle thee,
Thy form beloved will not in air dissolve.

PERCIVAL.

Griselda!

GRISELDA.

Percival! Now all is well.
Yes, all is well again! Within the depths
Of the wide ocean of forgetfulness
My sorrows die away with all their waves;
My lord and master, mine, once more, thou art,
Mine art thou, mine, and mine alone thou art,
Within thy loving arms warm glows my heart!

### PERCIVAL.

O were I still thy husband and thy lord!

### GRISELDA.

What say'st thou?   What?   O frenzy of my soul,
That mingles empty dreamings with the real!
Bewildered senses, learn to find your way,
And separate what has been from what is.

### PERCIVAL (*aside.*)

Defy her tears, and steel thyself, my heart!

### GRISELDA.

My honored lord, I know thou hast forgiven
The tumult blind that conquered and misled me;
My fate stands clearly now before my eyes,
And well thy kindness do I recognize!
Thou camest hither as my comforter,
With words compassionate, with gentle words,
To drop as oil and balsam on my wounds.
Receive my thanks for them!

### PERCIVAL.

        Hear me, Griselda;
Not gentle pity guided me to thee;

The day of retribution dire has come;
I share the fate that drove thee from thy home.
I am accused of treason by the King;
I am proscribed, my feudal rights withdrawn;
Pursued, the outlaw's brand upon my brow,
I wander forth, the spy upon my track;
My head just ready for his murderous grasp.

### GRISELDA.

A banished and imperilled fugitive!
Thy precious life in danger and I live?
And thou dost tarry here, dost dare to linger,
When life and freedom every moment threatens?
Fly! Fly!

### PERCIVAL.

      In vain!   All points are closely guarded,
Escape there is none, every hope is lost.

### GRISELDA.

Oh, then, give light to me, thou Fount of grace;
Him must I save, help me, Almighty God!

### PERCIVAL.

Thou wilt save him who took away thy boy,
To give the King, who roughly thee disowned,
And snatched away all that thy life adorned?

### GRISELDA.

Was it thy will to agonize my heart?
Is this the time to ponder on my fate
When trembles *thine* upon destruction's edge?
Come, even if an army should oppose me,
I thee must rescue, and, by heaven, I will!

### PERCIVAL.

Cease, cease!  Thy ruin is involved in mine,
The only purchase of my life is thine.

### GRISELDA.

O that thy words were true; that I might give
My life for thine, might for thy safety die!
The tie that made us one is rent in twain,
Yet still this heart is thine!  No more on thine
Can it contented rest, in ecstacy
No more upon thy breast o'erflow with joy;
Nor open up to thee its hidden depths;
But break for thee, yes, break for thee it can!

### PERCIVAL.

Nay, cease!  I'll to the fate that beckons me!
There, in the thicket, is the gleam of arms.

GRISELDA (*hastily.*)

'Tis they; away with you! Q fly!   Have mercy
Upon my death-like anguish!   Fly and hide!
Thou know'st the cavern deep within the wood,
Whose entrance, by the ivy, is concealed,
It was my childhood's play-ground, and to thee,
My dearest husband, I confide its secret;
Within its deep recesses hide thyself,
Or thou wilt see me lifeless at thy feet!
Fly to it, Percival!   There's safety there!

PERCIVAL (*pressing* GRISELDA *passionately to his heart.*)

Griselda! Angel! Saviour!

GRISELDA.

Fly! oh fly!

[PERCIVAL *hastens away;* GRISELDA *watches him till
    he disappears in the thicket, then sinks down upon
    her knees, raises her hands to heaven, and says :*
Save him, my God, let me the victim be!

SCENE IV.—GINEVRA *appears in the background with*
ORIANA, LANCELOT, GAWAIN, *and their attendants:*
GRISELDA *springs up.*

### GINEVRA.

This was the path he took; his traces follow!
Search through the brushwood! Range along the brook!
Sir Gawain, make in yonder hovel inquest!
Hasten! He must be found!

[GAWAIN *and armed men go.*

GINEVRA (*stepping up to* GRISELDA.)

Ha! Answer thou!
To thee he came! We bid thee tell us truly
Whither he fled and where conceals himself?

### GRISELDA.

Whom seek'st thou, Queen?

### GINEVRA.

Nay, thou canst deceive me
With no pretence of feigned simplicity.
I know thee, who thou art, as thou know'st me;
Thou art Griselda, wife of Percival!
For him, the flying traitor, we make search;
To us do thou his hiding-place reveal.

6

GRISELDA.

I, Queen, reveal it?

GINEVRA.

Here, to thee, he came;
Thou knowest where he fled.

GRISELDA.

And if I know,
I am Griselda, wife of Percival!

GINEVRA.

Thou, traitoress, dost hide his guilty head;
Deny it not; I know it and have seen it!

GRISELDA.

God saw it too, and of the fugitive
His clouds conceal the trace!   His guardian angel
And friendly night, protect him from his foes.

GINEVRA.

Bid not defiance to the higher powers!
Presume not thou to conflict wage with Kings!
We, as a net-work, have arranged our forces,
Nor for his safety silence shall avail,
But to thine own destruction it shall lead.
For if to us thou wilt not him betray,
Ere moments fly thy life shall ransom pay!

GRISELDA.

Here it is; take it!

GINEVRA.

By the heavens above,
Is this the woman, who without resistance,
Obeying, like the maid, her master's nod,
Gave up her child, gave up and left her home?

LANCELOT.

In vain are thy endeavors!   Cease, Ginevra,
The heart that loves knows not the fear of death.

GINEVRA.

A lofty spirit in this woman dwells,
The hopes and dreams I cherished, she dispels.
(*To* ORIANA.)
Speak thou to her!   To shake her purpose try!

ORIANA.

Griselda, hear me!   Did not Percival
Thy child deliver over to the King,
And to ally himself to nobler birth
Not thrust thee helpless, poor, and naked out?

And from the very summit of the bliss
To which he bore thee up in dizzy flight,
To sudden ruin headlong cast thee down?
Did he not so?

### GRISELDA.

So did he, as thou say'st!

### ORIANA.

And thou for love such sacrifice canst make,
Canst crush the dread of dying, for its sake;
But was it real then? Loved thee Percival?
Into thy power his fate has bid him fall,
Wilt thou his life who took from thine its all?

### GRISELDA.

O not in strict proportions measure love!
Why, what is love, then, if it nothing gave
More than itself received, if it endured
No more than it required, if it not,
Like a strong rock, resisted angry winds;
If, as Hope's final refuge, in misfortune
It kept not true and steadfast, what were love?
I revelled in the light of his renown,
Shall I forsake him when his fortunes frown?

### LANCELOT.

Her soul is like the heaven's transparent blue,
And blessed in its dazzling, glorious hue,
Like lightly-floating angels, dwell her thoughts.

### GINEVRA.

Bring hither chains and fetters; bind her fast!
Repeat thy prayer, thy life is at its last.

### GRISELDA.

Here am I, Father! Take this stricken life
Home to Thyself, and let my soul return
Back to the source from which at first it sprang,
Rising from out the mouldering dust of death;
And if it bear the mark of earthly stain,
Its humble aspirations, Lord, Thou know'st;
Receive it as a Father true and kind;
I have loved much, and much Thou wilt forgive.

### LANCELOT.

Vain the attempt with fraud her to ensnare,
For love keeps watch and bids her heart beware.

### GINEVRA.

There lies a magic sweetness in her words,

That trembles through and overwhelms my soul.
(*To* ORIANA.)
He conquers! Never will I break this heart.

---

SCENE V.—GAWAIN *returns with his attendants, who bring* CEDRIC *with them.*

### GAWAIN.

We have fulfilled thy bidding, gracious Queen :
This blind man was the hovel's only inmate,
And thou canst question him thyself, my lady.

### GRISELDA.

My father! Oh, my God, it is my father !

### GINEVRA.

Her father ! Ah, then, all is not yet lost !
(*To* GRISELDA.)
Look hither, and the truth no more deny !
He shares thy fate ! Wilt thou behold him die?

### GRISELDA (*kneeling*).

Oh, Queen ! Have mercy on his hoary hair,
His short and fleeting years remaining spare,

Until God's angel touch his blinded eyes,
And unto light eternal bids him rise.

#### LANCELOT.

No longer torture her !   Desist, Ginevra !

#### GRISELDA (*in an agony of excitement.*)

O let compassion's gentle grace decide !
Threaten no more this fading life and dim,
Lead me, lead me to death, but pardon him !

#### GINEVRA.

Speak and he lives !   Thy silence only slays him !

#### GRISELDA (*after severe mental conflict.*)

Protect him then, ye angels !   Speak I may not !
> [*She sinks fainting to the ground.*

#### GAWAIN.

She faints !

#### LANCELOT.
> O hold her up !

#### CEDRIC.
> What has befallen ?

Bewildering sounds unto mine ears are borne !
O that the veil from off mine eyes were torn !

GINEVRA.

Bear her away! We're conquered, Oriana!
Though I with blushes own it, yet I ween
Of England's wives I've the most loyal seen.
Bear her away! And with her, yon old man,
To Pendennys! Oh, how I glow with shame!
Before the collier's daughter I must kneel;
Conceal me, darkness; hide, eternal night!

CEDRIC (*as he is led off*).

O when will clemency abide with might?

# FIFTH ACT.

Scene I.—*Castle Pendennys*—Ronald *and other serv-ants are engaged in covering the estrade with carpets and adorning the hall with garlands, etc.*

### Ronald.

Quick to the work, my comrades, dally not!
Display the splendor of this carpet's hues
Before the royal throne.

### One of the Servants.

The royal throne?

### Ronald.

What is there so amazing?   And why stretch
The yawning chasm of thy throat so wide?
Didst thou not see the King, when mounted high,
He rode within th' enclosure of these walls?

### Servant.

The huntsman in a common doublet green,
That was the King?

### RONALD.

      Thou fool! Do kings wear crowns
Upon their heads when they go forth to hunt?
Here lay a carpet also for the Queen!

### ANOTHER SERVANT.

Mean you the beauteous dame in scarlet robes,
Who rode upon the white and ambling steed?

### RONALD.

How dares the fellow prate of ambling steeds,
Of beauteous ladies and of scarlet robes?
Art thou the man to dare to raise thine eyes
To look upon a Queen when thee she passes?
More garlands there, more garlands there, I say
O'er yonder wall! Like the green woods in May
Adorn this hall, and with a fragrance sweet
And bridal splendor do thou make it full.

### A THIRD SERVANT.

Can it be, Ronald? Thinks our lord so soon
Of taking him a wife?

### RONALD.

      Thou blinded fool!
Didst thou not see our lady back return?

Will not her living breath flow gently yet
Within the splendid halls of Pendennys?
Is not Griselda still the mistress here?


### SERVANT.

Ay, back returned she, but it was in chains
That by her father's side she hither came.


### RONALD.

You stupid fellows!   Can you then conceive
Only of things that you can touch and feel,
Distinguish not the semblance from the real,
Man from his dress, the kernel from the shell?
More wreaths, I tell you, upon yonder wall!
Spare not the ornament of foliage green!
O if my tongue no solemn promise bound,
You would break forth in shouts, and heaven's high arch
Would with your jubilee reverberate.


### ONE OF THE SERVANTS.

What know'st thou?   Say!


### ANOTHER.

Ay, Ronald, tell it us!

### RONALD.

I out of school tell tales? Not I indeed!
More wreaths, I tell you! Make the table ready,
Off to the kitchen, down into the cellar!
Away! Away with you, ye laggard men!
A day like this will ne'er return again!

---

### SCENE II.—LANCELOT *and* GAWAIN *appear, and the servants gradually retire to the background.*

### GAWAIN.

What, you would leave us? Would withdraw yourself
From the Queen's favor, from the royal court?

### LANCELOT.

Turned from its purpose, changed is all my heart,
And I awake as from a troubled dream.
In these few days much have I lived to see!
The chains are broken that have fettered me:
The greatest charm, I feel it, is not beauty,
Nor sparkling wit the soul's best attribute!
Not spots upon my sun can I endure,
Nor rust upon the mirror of my honor;
Farewell, then, au revoir!

### GAWAIN.

                    Sir Lancelot,
Griselda's tortures have your soul beclouded;
But now the pressure of her grief is o'er.
Remain and see her festival, her triumph.


### LANCELOT.

Truly these walls show festival array,
And blooming garlands every pillar grace;
'Twere a less trifling task to deck a soul,
And for a festal scene adorn its depths!
Farewell, Sir Gawain, I am forced from hence!


### GAWAIN.

Most bitterly the Queen will you regret.


### LANCELOT.

Perhaps; but time will teach her to forget.
Impatient in the court-yard stamps my steed,
Across the sea to France, the waves shall bear me—
Conceal not from her, Gawain, why I part;
And if within her breast thus meet again
The evil spirits, haughtiness and pride,
Of Lancelot remind her and Griselda.          [*Goes.*

### GAWAIN.

He goes! 'Twere well, fcr once, mine oath attests,
If tears should come as uninvited guests
To the dark glowing eye of Dame Ginevra.

---

## SCENE III.—GAWAIN, PERCIVAL, *and* TRISTAN.

### PERCIVAL.

Now from deception's burden I 'm relieved,
Torn is the net-work that my heart ensnared;
The day of expiation is achieved,
The tested one for triumph is prepared.
To paint her virtues words are all too poor!
Th' offences of my youth I here abjure,
Wide as the boundless heavens my love shall be,
A halo shall surround her, in a sea
Of pure delight her life shall float away.
The only tears that henceforth shed she may,
Shall fall when for some broken rose she's grieved.
If she has known the depths of sore distress,
She shall forget it all in happiness!

### TRISTAN.

Well will it be for you should this be so :
If flight of days bring healing on its wings,
As fans bring cooling as they come and go.
But much I fear me that these depths profound
Will leave their scar as they have felt their wound.

### PERCIVAL.

Upon love's magic power let me depend,
Let her heart own me as its dearest friend,
And undisturbed and calm to mine adhere.
Deep-rooted is the pain, high rules the joy,
When to her bosom she shall clasp her child,
When in my eager arms she shall be pressed,
Peace will once more find home within her breast,
To her pale cheek the roses will return.
Will not her praises every lip prolong,
To be re-echoed in the minstrel's song,
And sounded forth in ages yet to come ?
She shall become a holy saint to me,
My life to hers shall consecrated be ;
And as the moon her changing light renews,
So new and endless joys for her shall live ;
She loves me, Tristan, and she will forgive !
Sir Gawain, tell me, what delays the Queen ?
She gave her word, when will it she redeem ?

### GAWAIN.

As white and red upon her cheek contend,
So in her soul there for dominion strives
Duty with shame, with weakness firm resolve,
And dizzy by these fluctuations made,
She strives for strength, and in despair she clings
To a stray word that proves to be a straw,
Till in the whirlpool of her thoughts she sinks.

### PERCIVAL.

She gave her word, and hesitates to keep it?

### GAWAIN.

She will and she will not.　Griselda's triumph
Her inmost soul has shaken to its depths,
Ashamed she recognizes all her worth,
And gladly at her feet would bow the knee.
But what her heart doth counsel wills not she,
And yet she must consent; King Arthur presses
For the fulfillment of her word; commands,
And not entreaties, are his earnest words;
And when I left her seemed it her desire
With dignity to yield her to her fate;
And see, now see, she hither comes apace.

### PERCIVAL.

'Tis she !   Have you my men assembled all ?

### GAWAIN.

It has been done.

### PERCIVAL.

      And brought you back my boy,
Sir Tristan, brought you him within these walls ?

### TRISTAN.

Safe within Ronald's arms I placed the child.

### PERCIVAL.

Then all is well !   Take breath again, my soul,
Now strikes the glorious moment of my life.

---

SCENE IV.—*Sound of trumpets from without ;* KING
 ARTHUR *and* GINEVRA *in royal garments ;* ORIANA,
*Knights, and Ladies, followed by* PERCIVAL'S *retinue,*
*enter in festal procession.*

### KING ARTHUR.

In hospitable guise, Sir Percival,
The walls of Pendennys have welcomed us ;
Yet we without reserve will make confession,

That we were led to cross this friendly threshold
Less by the wish to seek thee in thy home,
Than to adjust the odious, hateful feud
'Twixt one with worth, and one with pow'r endued,
From tests severe to shield the good and true,
And shelter love from the misuse of power!
Yet sorrowing we learn that to the hour
Was brought the victim sought by senseless pride,
And that defiance wicked did provide.

### PERCIVAL.

As thou hast said, so is't, my lord and King!
The sacrifice was made, the victory won;
Not thoughtlessly have I the strife begun,
I have brought home to me the pearl of wives,
My words have been confirmed; and now for yours!
The garland she has won in conflict dread,
Wreathe, green and graceful, round Griselda's head,
And lowly at her feet the Queen must kneel.

### KING ARTHUR.

Here stands she! Speak to her!

### GINEVRA.

          My lord and husband!
It was a royal word I pledged to him,
And royally Ginevra will redeem it!

### King Arthur.

Now then, what wait we for ?   The moment flies,
Unto the victor let us yield the prize !
Go, and bring hither Cedric and Griselda !
(Aside to Ginevra.)
Ginevra, if the splendor of our crown
Is by this day's humiliation marred,
We must esteem our fate as well-deserved,
Not that we in thy fault have taken share,
But that we from it had not thee preserved !

> [King Arthur *and* Ginevra *descend from the
> throne ;* Percival *retires into the background
> with his vassals.*

---

Scene V.—Griselda *enters in a woolen dress and
apron, leading* Cedric.

### Cedric.

Tell me, Griselda, whither dost thou lead me ?
Is it to death?
King Arthur.
Fear not, old man, step nearer ;
Thy King and master speaks to thee—Griselda !

Be not surprised that these familiar walls
From whence but now thou wast an outcast thrust,
Adorned in splendor do thy coming greet,
Whom festal pomp and circumstance should meet;
Rejoice thou also in thy welcome home.

### GRISELDA.

What say you, Sire?   Do you the truth announce?
Both fear and hope contend within my soul,
And with confusion all my thoughts perplex!
Is Percival no longer under ban?
Extinguished is the hatred of thy heart?
For me in splendor are these walls arrayed?

### KING ARTHUR.

By England's crown, I but the truth announce.

### GRISELDA.

The words upon thy lips are words of peace,
Not anger's thunder, not revenge's shriek;
The high-born lady seated at thy side
No longer hurls upon me thunderbolts,
But gentle smiles illuminate her face.
O, if it is the truth thou makest known,
Then see me supplicating at thy feet,
And give a gracious hearing to my prayer!

### CEDRIC.

Entreat them not! They listen not to prayers!

### KING ARTHUR.

Not kneeling speak to me! Arise, Griselda!
Whate'er thou askest I will freely grant,
And never my protection shalt thou want.

### GRISELDA.

I plead not for myself, my lord and King,
It is for Percival I make entreaty;
Let the full spring-tide glory of thy grace
Irradiate, as erst it did, his brow;
Restore to him his power and his domains,
To him restore them, Sire, not to me!
Well know I my deserts, and that my place
Was never in a proud and titled house.

### CEDRIC.

And therefore, silly fool, he cast thee out!

### KING ARTHUR.

Griselda! Shame would gladly truth conceal,
That duty bids us to reveal to thee.
Learn then, thou wast deceived by mere pretence;
We did not tear thy child from out thine arms.

Our will did not your marriage bond annul ;
No royal danger threatened Percival.
The terrors that o'erwhelmed thee, are not, were not,
What made thee tremble was a shadow only.

### GRISELDA.

What say you?   Mere pretence—an empty shadow?
My child, my Percival, but mere pretence?
All I endured?   The agony I nourished
With my heart's-blood until it was consumed!
A mere pretence?   Shed light upon this darkness!
With eager yearnings thirst I for the truth!

### CEDRIC.

What, we by mere illusions were entangled?

### ORIANA.

A word, Griselda, will explain this riddle,
And lift the veils that now obscure thy sight.
Thy whole experience was a passing jest,
That Percival, the rogue, upon thee played.
A mummery ; the occasion was a wager,
The prize—was but the footfall of a Queen,
And in the bargain was thrown in thy tears!
This was his sole intent, with pride to prove

The collier's daughter worthy of his love,
Degenerate in birth, but not in blood.


CEDRIC.

For that? For that? Oh shameless, wanton act,
In floods of bitter tears to try the heart!


[PERCIVAL *makes his way through the crowd, and
throws himself at* GRISELDA'S *feet.*


PERCIVAL (*entreatingly.*)

Belovèd, art thou angry? O forgive me!
Wipe from the tablet of thy memory
The signs and tokens of thy sufferings;
Let thy face beam with reconciliation,
And in th' abyss of an exhaustless love
Sink the remembrance of my great offence.


GRISELDA (*steps back, she looks for a moment expressively
at* PERCIVAL, *then speaks like one awaking from a
dream :*)

A passing jest! Repeat it! Let me hear it
From thy lips, Percival! Answer me truly,
Was it a test alone, was it a jest?

PERCIVAL (*after a short pause.*)

'Twas as thou say'st, a test.   But it is over !
Thy child is safe restored, thy father free,
Thy happiness is all to thee restored !
Forgive thou me !   Reflect not on the jest
That proved thee faithful !   It is over now ;
Let it forgotten and forgiven be.

GRISELDA.

A jest, and I—

> [*She presses her hand passionately upon her heart
> for some moments ; then covers her eyes with
> both hands, stands some seconds silent, half-
> turned away, then says :*

'Twas a hard jest, and rich in bitter tears !

PERCIVAL.

Thou weepest still !   O let thy tears be dried.
My choice of thee they ventured to deride
Because the forest bore thee, and because
Thy beauteous form was framed in poverty ;
Then I opposed to title and to rank,
Thy heart so innocent, thy mind so pure !
Through sharpest pains I ventured thee to lure ;
And thou hast triumphed, triumphed in each test.

Ginevra in the dust to thee must kneel,
And England with thy praises shall resound !
Wilt keep thine anger 'mid such high renown ?

GINEVRA (*who, meanwhile, has descended, with* KING
ARTHUR, *from the throne.*)

He speaks the truth, Griselda !   I confess
The share in his offence which on me rests :
What he fulfilled was planned alone by me,
We have repentance won, thou victory ;
And freely we proclaim, our word redeeming,
In face of England's noblemen and knights,
That regal splendor fades before thy worth,
That if the good and true on earth took rank,
Thou queen wouldst be, and England's crown wouldst
    wear ;
And at thy feet Ginevra humbly kneels ;
Forgive the pain that reckless pride has caused !

PERCIVAL (*in proud joy.*)

She kneels !   Let it resound through forests wild,
Ginevra kneels before the collier's child !

GRISELDA.

O Queen !   Arise !   I plead with thee !   Arise !
Thou shalt not kneel before the collier's child !

   7

The victory's mine, let me refuse the prize
That torture and deception won for me!
About my head you would the laurel weave,
But I have won instead a crown of thorns;
For all the death-like anguish I endured
Grows pale before the darkness of this hour.
Faith went forth with me in my woolen dress,
When with deluded steps I left these halls;
Now the delusion flies, but faith flies too.


PERCIVAL.

What?   Has thine eye no single glance of love,
Thy lips no more a smile for Percival?
What pride has forfeited, let love repay;
Give to the winds thy sorrows, let the morning
Bid darkness vanish at its cheerful dawning.
If I a cup of wormwood offered thee,
Now sweetest draughts of joy I mingle up;
Thy life shall be a crown of blooming flowers;
Thy heart's most sacred and most secret wish,
I into glad reality will turn;
Fulfillment of thy dreams I'll undertake,
And scarcely shall a silent yearning wake,
Ere longing and possession shall be one;
And as the ocean circles round this isle,

So waves of pure delight shall round thee run,
And memory of the past shall thee beguile.

GRISELDA (*wearily, and in a broken voice.*)
What thou hast promised that thou may'st not give !
No joy will henceforth in this bosom live,
Nor pleasure ever animate this face !
Can this poor life by glory be made bright ?
Not rank and power, love only can delight !
O thou hast gambled all my peace away !
This faithful heart was but a toy to thee ;
Hast bound me to the stake, and made display
To other eyes of my soul's misery !
Thou didst not tremble lest I sink therein,
Thy only fear was lest the Queen should win !
May God forgive thee, as I thee forgive !
But thou, my father, say, is the offence
Of which thou didst accuse me, paid for now ?
If my excess of love became a crime,
And found a god in him the child of clay,
Have I not made atonement with my tears,
With the deep grief of my deluded soul ?
Once more with loving arms may I embrace thee,
Dare sink upon the heart whence love me stole,
Not longing pomp and station to acquire,
An impulse high, not passionate desire ?

### CEDRIC.

Come, my poor child, rest on thy father's heart,
Drink healing from the copious fount of love
That springs within it unadulterate.

### GRISELDA.

O lead me forth into my native woods,
And to the friendly shelter of our hut.
Let me lay dreamily on nature's breast
This heart that has been wounded unto death,
And in the shadow of her moss-grown trees,
Let her beloved one fade away and die.

### CEDRIC.

Come, come, my child; with blushes let them say,
Pain bore she, with affront could not away.

### PERCIVAL.

My very heart stands still; thy words, Griselda,
Have stirred the deep abysses of my soul;
But yet thy serious face deceives me not;
Wilt thou requite me for the wrong I did
With gloomy threats, provokingly embitter
My exultation in my victory?
O do it not! Be reconciled to me!
More radiant will thy crown triumphant be
If love and kindness are thy sole revenge.

### GRISELDA.

O Percival, I see thee through my tears,
And the lip trembles that shall greeting give;
Yet speak I must, this must decided be,
Frank must it be; peace dwells in honesty!
My heart was thine, but never understood;
And in thy hand it broke! For thou couldst play
With its pure warmth, and thou couldst vaunt thyself
On its devotion, on its constancy!
Thou hast not loved me! It has vanished far
The glad and sweet illusion of my life.
My Paradise has into ruins fallen;
A desert looks me joyless in the face!
I can no longer with thee hand in hand,
When heart from heart turns wearily away,
I cannot, Percival! My whole life hangs,
My self-respect, my only aspiration,
Upon the god-like image of my dreams,
Upon thine image! O let me preserve it,
As bright, untarnished once it filled my soul!

### PERCIVAL.

What are thou thinking of, wilt what achieve?

### GRISELDA.

If in obscurity, was I but born
To be the sport of arbitrary will,

A ball to win and lose upon a throw?
Thou hast not loved me; without love to thee,
Should I be worthy to become thy wife
Or to remain such? Percival, thou know'st
On thee, and on thee only, hangs my heart!
Unto the lowly house that gave me birth,
Return I now, and to the forest shades,
And as their whispers were my cradle-songs,
My funeral dirge shall murmur in their glades.

### PERCIVAL.

Forsake me, wilt thou, thou wilt fly from me?
Mine art thou, mine! who dares set claim on thee?
I hold thee fast, who dares thee tear away?
Who from thy marriage vow has freed thee, say?

### GRISELDA (*suppressing her tears*).

Thyself! The bond of love was rent by thee,
And we must separate! Yes, it must be!
Permit me only but to keep my boy
Till the short remnant of my life is o'er.
For well I know my days are nearly spent,
And as the parting swallow upward flies,
So homeward soars the sorrow-laden soul!
Then as my legacy do thou receive him;

Of knightly honor teach him the career;
To him atone for thine offence to me!
But in the bloom of life do thou remain,
A noble stock, of glorious renown,
And if the force of love should thee constrain
Thy days with marriage ties anew to crown,
O be not moved by evil powers, to dare
Also to lay anew this testing snare,
For love's sake only love could pardon it!

[*She goes slowly away with* CEDRIC.


PERCIVAL (*steps in her way.*)

Griselda, thou wouldst leave me? Nay, thou shalt not!
Thou dar'st not! Stay, Griselda!


KING ARTHUR (*waving him back*).

                    Hold! Fall back,
Sir Percival, henceforth I will protect her;
Thy rights were forfeit when thou didst reject her,
And now unhindered shall she homeward turn.
Love, for love's sake, will every conflict bear;
But bids the barbarous impulse to beware
That fain upon her head would set its heel!

Thy house is empty, happiness has fled,
The bow of vict'ry's triumph vanishéd !
Now dwell within thy vacant halls alone,
Sufficient to thyself, and into ruins thrown !

> [*The* KING *departs with his followers and the vas-
> sals of* PERCIVAL, *who with his face concealed
> in his hands, remains alone in the foreground.*

THE END.